Jennifer's Travels

Moonscapes of Recombobulation

by Jennifer Darland

Arts of Earth and Sky

For Tree

Also by Jennifer Darland

The Answer Wheel:

360 Illuminations for the Human Spirit

Bridge between Temple and Dream:

Poems from Lonely Nature

Jennifer's Travels
Moonscapes of Recombobulation
Contents

A Note from Jennifer

The Moonscapes that follow are surreal dreams experienced over the course of one summer during an intense season of deep healing and change.

These travels are strange but authentic, and the transient power of such immense dreaming was exclusive to this single summer.

Though vivid and mind-altering, these trippy recollections were not drug induced. In fact, this period was one of complete sobriety.

It was a time to shapeshift, to recombobulate the chaos within, to dismantle and reassemble body and soul from the depths of dream.

1. Bull Hide

I am lying on the front lawn of a place that I feel more comfortable going than my own home and I am happy I get to spend the entire night here…this is rare. The only reason I am allowed to do so is because there is a ceremony to be held and I have a job in it since I previously offered to volunteer.

I lay on the lawn with my arms crossed behind my head, stretched out on my back. My legs are held up above me by a hammock that cannot support my entire body because of the giant hole in the middle.

I roll around and my shirt colors seep into the grass and I am encouraged to continue by some men sweeping a mass area of concrete adjacent to me. It starts to get dark and nearly all the grass has been painted with the outlines of my clothes, so I stop and return to my relaxed position of lying on the lawn. I feel many hands tenderly massaging me, but despite the softness it somehow hurts so I tell them to stop. They do, but then they rise from the ground beneath me wearing my clothes that I painted into the lawn.

The men who were sweeping the cement area are taking a break and one yells, "On your marks!" and the men wearing my clothes run onto the cement surface and form an outline around the perimeter of the area. A parade of people wearing ponchos wrapped around them lead cows and bulls onto the cement platform. The cement drops and all of the people, cows, and bulls disappear and I am still in the yard, completely alone.

Two bulls run fast from behind me and quickly pass on either side of me and abruptly stop from full speed right before me. They turn around and each has a black hawk in their mouth. Falling from the sky on a large block of cement, a man announces that the bulls will now fight to determine which life should be spared. The bulls drop the hawks, jerk their heads violently back, and both bite me just beneath my heart. I feel burning and I know it's venomous…I see the venom eating away at their lips as it drips and my skin deteriorates where the contaminated saliva drops from the bite.

The man announcing the battle, still repeating the announcement, descends from the sky and puts me on the flat top of a tree on a large leaf as he floats in midair beside me on his concrete piece. As I rest on the tree, he slabs wet concrete on my flesh-eating venomous outbreak. It rapidly heals and he shoots the bulls with an arrow from our place up high. He goes down to the ground, pulls the hides from their bodies, and throws them at me. I don't catch them, so they fall down the tree through the branches alongside the trunk and land on the lowest layer of branches near the ground below.

Solidifying in form into my concrete mold, I fall down in the path of where the hides had just fallen and land in a hammock at the bottom. The hammock stings like hot venom so I lay on the ground beneath it…comfortable in my motionless form, waiting for the heat ceremony to begin. Hopefully this cement will melt.

2. Stone Jelly

I am still and immoveable like a boulder, looking down a long dirt path that spirals all around…it comes in front of me, around me, and beyond me past where I can see. I hear a thundering rumble coming up the path and it quickly draws nearer, becoming louder every second. I see a perfectly smooth round stone the size of a large animal tumbling towards me. Though I can not move, I know I hold the important duty of covering a jelly substance that was given to me to guard some time ago.

This jelly has expanded in quantity and has risen over me, binding me to the rocky ground. It jiggles from time to time when the Earth below us rumbles. With all my might, I pull myself away from the jelly to see further into the oncoming situation.

I rise from a stone, separating from it segment by segment, as I take notice of my caterpillar-like form…more specifically, my long gooey black figure that is so long it takes eons to go anywhere with this section by section chain reaction I must move myself by. I accept my form, moving on from my immoveable state that seems to have lasted centuries, and I turn myself away from the path of the oncoming stone.

I am safely out of the way and I turn my head to see the massive rolling rock pave a path of destruction where I had just been. Plant parts and animal remnants are sticking to it, and I notice the rock has rolled over the gel that remains dependent upon my guardianship…and that it is enabling the stone to capture pieces of the nature around me. Without thought I accept my responsibility to retain the gel, to both fulfill my promise, and to protect the apparent theft of nature that is occurring.

I elevate in my lanky caterpillar-like state and the small hairs lining my back morph into long eyelashes that extend far out before me, pointing my sight to specific things far ahead, my long distance vision having been greatly strengthened. I view a greater distance than I could have dreamed and before I know it, I have feet racing below me, throwing me into my eye's path. Hair is still growing out of me as I dash faster in the strong wind that pushes in my speed's favor from behind, propelling my large jackrabbit-like feet further towards the round stone that still disrupts the path as it rolls far ahead. My head is moving up and down like I am diving into the air, maximizing my acceleration as I experience perfect harmony with the wind.

I am almost to the stone now, moving at top speed, sure to catch it. I see a body of water ahead that I wish to drink from, but I must catch the stone and recover the jelly first. The stone jolts to a halt, and unable to slow down in time, I plow into it. It does not hurt but now I have bounced off and I'm falling through the air towards the water, which is much lower than I originally observed. I feel the jelly all around me as I scratch the itch on my neck with my chin, finding this the only part of me moveable besides the parts of me that have no choice…the parts swinging through the air as I surrender to the fall, both thankful and relieved I got the jelly. I involuntarily tense up, preparing for the high impact onto the water, and splash! I go in feeling much less pain than I anticipated. I am relieved and no longer out of breath as I was for quite some time prior to this moment. But now I am at ease and I feel oxygen and water permeate me entirely.

I devour a tadpole as soon as I see it, and by my motions and the absence of my recently acquired mammalesque legs, I realize that I am now a fish. A frog looks up to me from the bottom surface underwater with eyes longing for her baby, whom I had just eaten. My stomach churns with remorse and I feel great pressure from above until I crash into the bottom next to the frog. The stone has fallen and is just about to collide into the bottom, which will certainly demolish the environment I have found myself in. I push the frog out of the way and the stone falls, causing harm to some snails who are crushed entirely. I recover the snails as a snack for the frog and I, giving most to her, leaving some for myself. She smiles and swims away. I look back to the stone and see more jelly on its surface as it breaks loose into the water, putting long faces on the fish nearby.

I touch the water-diluted gel on the rock, which instantly turns me into a frog with the ability to jump high, having superb control of my arms and legs. I see some seaweed far above and with a great leap, I collect four strands and tie them around the stone. I find a large seashell with a hole in its center, and tie each end of the seaweed through it. I hear a pleasant soft voice emitting from the shell, so I hold it to my ear. The shell sucks me into it…the seaweed and stone following, all glazed with a bit of jelly.

I look down to find myself standing on the large stone on a sandy beach, overlooking water decorated with sailboats and floating logs. I glance down and see the rock has increased in size since I last saw it, and now I have the skinny clawed black feet of a sea gull. I see a black and orange beak protrude from my face and I dip it down to eat caterpillars on the surface. A piece of the stone chips off and tumbles down my throat into my stomach, launching me into flight. I cannot fly long because I feel the weight of the stone in my stomach, so

I land on one of the floating logs on the surface of the water.

People in a sailboat are amused by me and point, calling attention to one another. I sneeze and the stone spits out of me, impacting the forehead of one of the onlookers. This woman flies up into the air as she transforms into a bird and lands on the log right next to me. The man she was with, looking terribly panicked, jumps into the water swimming after her as our log floats away from his boat. As he reaches us, I see him holding the stone that I spat out, so I peck at his hand until I again acquire it. When I do, I feel myself sink into the water as I fluster to gain control…finding myself as a human.

I swim to shore looking back at the two sea gulls left behind on the log. I am naked but I'm holding stones to cover my private places with my legs slightly bent, one knee covering the other. Exhausted, I fall onto the sand, rolling around on top of the stones as they massage me. The tide comes in and the sand around me hardens, molding onto the stones, as they become one large form. It rolls away and circles itself oddly out of the way in order to crush me before continuing its path down the water's edge. I feel all of the bones in my human body break and the squishy substances beneath my skin squeeze out. I lay comfortably but unable to move, luxuriating in the pleasing pressure of the water as it rushes over me from time to time.

A voice coming from an invisible person speaks to warn me that he is going to drop something onto me momentarily and tells me not to panic. As promised, I feel a wet heavy drop splat onto me, and identify it by smell as the same gel that I have been dealing with. I feel the invisible human hand pick me up and scoop the fallen gel onto me…placing me and the substance on a rock, ensuring to contain as much of the jelly as possible. The rock swings me back and forth through the air by the side of the human, like I am being held in an invisible bag. Following the man, I am lifted onto a large horse and hang from his side…the invisible bag obviously tied around his neck.

We go to a deep spot in the forest after a long journey, where the man hops from his horse, and releases me from the sack. There is a square territory outlined with one layer of brick, with obliterated plants and fallen animals contained in it. The invisible man, a strong presence disguised in the veil of the air, tells me that these plants and animals were recovered from the stone just before it tumbled into the water after me…as I was falling far down before becoming a fish. He says he saw a creature like he'd never seen speeding towards the water, sure to drown, so he ran to stop him. He placed his hand to rest on the stone, he continues to explain, peeking over the edge to watch me…and in turn the gel bound him to its surface for many hours before he was released as an invisible man. Along with being invisible, he tells me, he was enabled go underwater and sneak into otherwise impossible places…and therefore has been following me. He says he has also been present with the stone since first touching it, and that it is growing in speed and size. He reminds me to not lose this jelly he has helped recover and is now leaving me

with, because the stone will be coming again…and only
I, alone, can touch the jelly that is bound to it.

3. Bound for Feeding

"Extra bands please, this one is extra long," I hear a man say as another tosses him an armful of large elastic bands. I feel the bands slip over my head and roll down my body until they sit wrapped around me, evenly spaced. I topple down with many more freshly wrapped bodies and join the pile of us at the bottom. The men who are wrapping us up and the ones standing guard at the bottom look almost identical to one another…pale skin with red eyes and prominent red gums highlighting their possessed smiles. I can not make out the details of the others who are banded like me because they are all covered in a thick tan balm that camouflages the features of their faces.

I recall the man asking for extra bands while binding me, so I look down at myself and at the others to compare sizes. My bundle does appear much longer than the rest, but peculiarly, it goes past where I feel like my feet are. I wiggle my toes to see if the bottom of the bundle moves, but the movement occurs towards the middle of it, as I expect. One of the men, watching us at our arrival spot at the bottom, whips his head around, noting my curiosity. His eyebrows turn downward towards the center of his face and he develops a gleaming scowl, locking my eyes into his…a warm wet sensation takes over my left foot and turns into a sharp pain as the insides of it drain from me.

I am in too much physical shock to move but my mind shows me the image of what is happening down below…a tiger has his teeth planted into my foot and is slowly drinking from me. The red eyed man I was staring at has redirected his focus to an unruly bound person who is kicking and fighting in attempt to break from their covering. The watchmen stomp on the ground and a chain link fence with barbed wire rises while many large wildcats run up to it from the other side, stopping at the fence.

One of the guards pushes the fence straight down onto the feisty captive, also covering a few others nearby, and pushes it as hard as he can into the bodies which then ooze back out in pieces from the openings in the fence. The big cats closest to the body fragments lick them up and when they are all consumed, the fence again rises, leaving the cats to wait for the next serving.

As the guard's attention remains elsewhere, I empty out from my body as I rise up and see myself laying beneath. I stop around the eye level of the dominating men and I wish to rise further, but it proves a struggle at first. I concentrate, keeping as tuned in as possible, and realize I must give up the familiarity of breathing to succeed. I consciously stop breathing and rise higher, sitting motionless in the air, studying the events below.

The pale red eyed men have holes on top of their heads and appear to be hollow inside. The cats look blurry from this high up and remain still and calm until the fence holes again bear shredded human meat. I squint my eyes to focus my vision and find holes on top of their heads as well. I look for the tiger from my bundle, wondering if he is behaving like the others. The watchmen still distracted, the tiger peeks out from the wrapping at the same moment I wonder about him. I continue to think of him after he retracts back into the bundle, and as I do, I feel him lick the wound he made on my foot that sits far below. He looks up at me and back again to the guards…then takes off at a high speed and my motionlessness in the air turns into a swift flight following after him. All I must do is watch the tiger run below and I drift at whatever needed pace to keep up with him, remaining directly above him.

Never turning, we reach an area saturated with tall chimneys and various pipes that penetrate the sky, thrusting smoke into it. Many rolls of people, bound as I was just some time ago, are prepared the same way…and the same red eyed men stand at the base of the tall chimneys. They are lined across from one another, turning iron rods up towards the top, transporting the wrapped people covered in tan balm to the hole from where the smoke emerges. One by one, the people are dropped into the smoke to fall down the chimney pipes. As they fall out, they are charred and pieces of them fall from their bodies to be licked up by large wildcats. Each cat then shoots out a pale man with red eyes and bright red gums from the top of its head, leaving a hole. Once the cat has a hole in its head, he runs away towards the scene we came from.

I observe this with no physical body to be detected by…I periodically check on the tiger who I arrived with, and we start conversing with each other silently through the space that separates us. As the conversation moves, I begin to feel that I am actually nowhere, just floating everywhere…I am in the tiger, in the air where I last remember feeling like I was, and even in the chimneys. The plan develops quickly and the tiger and I decide that he best scare away the naïve cats, innocent until they eat, while I drop his tiger fur into the hollow heads of the troublesome men, which he says will put them to sleep.

The last step is silently understood, without further conclusion or reiteration of the plan. The tiger charges into the operation, hissing and growling and throwing himself hysterically everywhere, instilling fear into all who witness. His size compounds with his roar and as planned, the other cats run away, their ears low and their stomachs close to the ground.   As this happens, I focus on dropping the tiger hair into the hollow heads of the men as I glide above, not remembering how I got the hair…but I have a surplus of it wrapped around me, and I simply relax to drop some down once I focus on where it needs to go.

The rods they turn to deliver the people high to the top of the chimneys slow down immediately as the hair goes inside of the men. Eventually the turning stops completely and the men fall asleep. The singed humans dispelled at the base move towards the sleeping men and slide into the openings in their heads. They wake in a panic, unwrapping their fellow humans that surround them. Many who were bound then stretch out and slip out of their bodies, which only I can see. Their fellow humans are bewildered at their sudden apparent death, as their bodies lay still behind them. Those who escaped from their bodies look my direction, as I also float formless in the air, and say "shhhh…" while they wisp by me, back towards the men and cats and the barbed wire fencing, where I left my own body.

The tiger summons me down and lets my spirit rest on his back as the wakened people sit in wonder, staring up at the multitude of tall chimneys. Pale men run towards us with a long barbed wire fence, and stop before me saying, "shhhh, it's us…" with unrestrained smiles. They say "one, two, three," and swing the fence into the air where it is broken to many pieces that each find their way down one of the chimneys. They turn to look at the tiger on whose back I am resting and smile with their modest expressions and pale blue or green eyes that were formerly red. They bow down to the tiger, and I confirm their hollow heads have been filled.

On the horizon ahead, I see many wildcats line up, still blurry. Once lined up they charge through an invisible boundary, erasing their blurriness as they cross it, and I see them all clearly. Each has a full fish or two in their mouths they set down at the base of the chimneys where the expelled bodies once lay. The rescued bound people and the revived perpetrators take part in the feast with the cats after an open invitation from them.

The tiger is most hungry, but before he eats, we run back to my body. He opens the bundle for me and I unite with my wounded flesh. He kneads his paws and rubs his head into my body, leaving his hair all over me. I fall asleep and wake up healed with the tiger at my foot, licking it as a last recovery step. The tiger seems hungry and like he has been waiting for me to wake for some time. He offers to put my body on his back for the journey to the others and the feast of fish, expecting me to still be rather sore from the foot draining. Instead, I leave my body to rest along with his, and both of our spirits rise into the sky. Moving in circles, instead of directly forward, we play in the sky until the feast is over…unable to feel hunger or fatigue, allowing the others to rejuvenate.

The fish has been consumed and the crowds disperse and the tiger and I are left at the chimneys, far from our bodies. Two men with red features and hollow heads remain walking the grounds, looking for people to capture. We sprinkle them with tiger hair that we both still hold until they fall asleep, when at once, we lift them up and drop them into the tallest chimney. They topple out burned and the group of wildcats returns to devour them.

The cats look up to see the spirits of the tiger and I, and run back to our bodies, pulling us along in the air above them. One black cat goes to the tiger and a spotted one goes to my body, and they each open their mouths to disclose meat they kept for us. They feed us and our bodies turn from gray to tan again and blood flow returns. I feel myself again in my body with my tiger companion licking my feet and both the black and spotted cats are above our heads, guarding us.

We walk away towards the chimneys, ready to dismantle them. A chain linked fence with barbed wire arises on the ground just before the chimneys as we finally approach them after the journey, much longer on foot. Together we charge into the fence, accepting the few wounds it creates, as it plummets into the tall chimneys, crushing them to the ground. Old fluids and chunks from inside the chimneys leak through the openings of the fence, and we lick it up which immensely fortifies us. The bands that the victims were bound with fall from the sky, attaching the fence and chimney remnants to the ground where they decay into the soil before our eyes. Red eyes and chunks of red gums scatter on top of the area and several tons of dirt fall from the sky, burying these things deep down…intending to never expose them again.

The tiger and I remember the men who brought up a fence by stomping on the ground, so we try it to investigate possibilities. At this, a nutritious food source grows, acceptable to cats and humans. From the fresh soil, a new population of humans and several types of cats arise…and together we wash the tan protective balm from the food before enjoying a continuous feast.

4. The Stairs are Right Now

I am spinning fast in circles with my arms out and my fingers are moving in a free rhythm, gently stroking the air. My spinning slows until I stop and I am grabbing onto the end of a large roll of paper. A piece breaks off as a message with an origami style paper lock, sitting atop it delicately to ensure it remains private until the recipient receives it. I look down at the astonishing detail of the design and as I touch it, clunky heavy wooden stairs drop down from its center, but each step looks ready to break anytime.

I run up them…certainly this is an invitation for me to deliver the message. I reach the top of the stairs and a dim light reveals only the shadows of the people piled on the top few stairs of the staircase. One silently moves up a couple of stairs to the top one that I am on and stands as close as he can without touching me, so I reach to hand him the message. He does not react, so I reach down for his hand to place the message in it. He appears to have no hands so I run off with the message looking to return down the stairs, but now I cannot find them.

The shadowy person comes to me again and snaps the message from my hands into his teeth and chews it. He swallows it and blows out a sphere of gum-like consistency, with the message in its original form inside of it. He blows it towards my mouth and I taste it for a moment, enjoying the sweet flavor, but then it pops and the message falls into my hands and another staircase drops before me.

I run up them with the message intact in my hand, the origami lock untampered. A floating king wearing a gold crown and a velvet purple robe comes down the stairs and greets me, looking slightly panicked. This message is of course intended for him, I think to myself, just when he takes a deep breath in and consumes the message into himself. The crown on his head grows and a necklace made of coins and small white flowers drops onto him and hangs far down his chest. He lifts it up to his pale face to smell the flowers and as he drops them to hang again, the message falls from his hands onto the ground. I pick it up and as I stand again the king is floating away, dragging the stairs he went down along with him, drifting far into the distance.

A princess comes from the site he disappeared into and drops many loose strands of grass into the area of land devastated by the dragging stairs the king hurriedly hauled away. As the grass fills the dirt void, the isle of dirt moves over and turns into a staircase. I grab her hand and take her with me up the staircase, and as we hold hands she takes us up to float in the air as we escalate up the new stairs. I am still holding the message and the princess and I start to hum in harmony with one another as the message floats away up the stairs just ahead of us. It approaches an open doorway at the end of the staircase, and pins itself onto the wall above it, and the door slams shut. I hear the princess and I hum inside the room behind the closed door, but now she is not floating near me and has gone away.

I see the message drop and start to slide under the closed door. After failing to pick it up from its tight fit with the ground, I push my fingers down as hard as I can, pressing it to the floor to keep it in place. The raised flower shape of the origami lock prevents the message from sliding under the door, so I relax the pressure in my hands. I no longer hear any noise coming from inside the room but I float again, spinning in the air. I drop and touch the origami tied message and the delicate circular lock protecting it turns and opens the door…parting it in the middle as half of the door slides open in each direction.

A staircase drops down and the message folds open across the top stair. The lock detaches from the message and bounces down, creating stair after stair. I look down to the message, a part of it exposed, and see a penciled sketch of a dismal staircase indicating downward motion, ready to collapse, and well built sturdy staircases going up. The fifth stair or so below me then entirely breaks away from the staircase, exposing people that were under each step as they float off into a sea of black, reaching in one last attempt to grab a stair that is still attached.

Two lift up from the fall and float in the air…a king in a purple robe, and a princess holding grass. The princess feeds the three of us some grass and the king takes off both his and the princess's crowns and tosses them to falling people who catch them and float up to us and beyond. I reach down, cupping my arms around the few stairs that remain, and flip them up to the floor I am on, turning them upside down. It is now a long upward staircase and the message rises to the top as I quickly follow. I reach the last stair at the top and see the people who rose after catching the crowns the king threw, cooking a pot full of food.

The princess and king, he still wearing his purple robe and she dressed modestly, arrive holding grass to throw into the pot. I reach into my pocket and throw bunches of flavorful herbs into the mix and the message jumps in after them and the stew starts to boil. I feel the heat and I spin to cool off in the chilly breeze my movement brings. As my vision focuses again from the blur of my spin, I see a spiral staircase built of twigs and mud supported by sturdy wood and stones, beautifully put together around us. The few of us dish up the stew and the many who were falling before. join us after running up the new staircase. I quietly sip my bowl, and a few sips in, part of the message is decipherable as it floats in the herby broth…it reads, "The stairs are right now."

5. Doorways of the Little People

The bottom half of me feels well moistened but the top of me feels crumbly and dry, like I might fall off of myself. I must get liquid to pour towards my head so instead of turning completely upside down, where I would indeed likely crumble, I lay flat on my back with my legs straight up in the air and arch my back. I rest my head backwards with my chin in the air, enjoying the relieving sensation, and after a few moments my legs feel like they are made of dominos flipping downwards towards my hips. I lift my head up in the midst of a quick reaction and see many small doors…rows of about five wide placed all the way up my leg, each door swinging open downwards toward the rest of me.

The doors in the layer closest to my root chakra bang down crashing open and I feel them impact me deep at the base of my spine. Behind each door is a small pocket, from which small men and women start running as they head from my legs to my core. The ones that do this collect themselves in a circle beginning above my belly button, moving down to where my legs start, and they face inward working together to open a large door that this area surrounds. Inside there are several small cups filled with a pale yellow green liquid and as the big heavy door swings open, the top of it hits my knees. My kneecaps pop off, releasing a downpour of clear water flowing heavy like a raging river. It crashes hard below into the cups, causing the yellow green liquid to splash out and cover my entire exterior.

My legs are still straight up and I can easily see inside of each door. The people who opened the door to the cups are still observing the event, so the door pockets they came from remain empty. The others contain a single large egg, functioning as the body of an oddly shaped person. At the top of each egg there are eyes and a normal human face with a few pieces of hair sticking out above. Each egg has a set of tiny bird-like legs that stand occasionally, but it is obviously difficult for their frail legs to support their large round bodies.

One I see is smearing the residual light yellow green liquid all over the interior pocket where he resides. Another one on the calf muscle of my other leg has pinchers instead of bird legs, and he is pinching the area inside his pocket, which I feel as a mild sting. One with the most hair, a black moppy mess, repeatedly rolls back and forth, knocking over small sticks that he sets up each time.

I shift my attention to another, close to my left ankle, and see bulging eyes that do not move. I cannot feel that part of my leg and I start to grow tired. Most of the doors on my legs are now shutting except this one displaying bulging staring eyes stays open. Before I nearly suddenly fall asleep, I reach to grab him but he bites me. I eventually open the door with the pincher man after many attempts due to its slipperiness from the yellow green shower. He constantly pinches with his crawfish-like parts so I hold him above the bulging eyed one until he is caught in the pinchers hold.

This happens quickly and I toss the biting man away from me, and coming out of nowhere, a gold chest slides over and opens in time to catch his egg body. I place the pinching accomplice back into his pocket and outline each door, hoping to permanently seal them, with the original yellowish contents of the cups that I find in random puddles. The substance rapidly flows downward towards my head and the clear water that replaced it bubbles out and upward from within to push it even further down my body. None stays around any of the doors as I intended, but instead rushes up towards the end of my head, wiping my face clean with it.

I hold my neck up gently and see that my entire chest and stomach are covered with open doors each displaying a miniature egg shaped person as my legs do, but these are nearly all quite a bit larger. These newly discovered ones on my core stay generally still but each holds a strong expression on their face. Two or three are mean and spitting burning sap into other pockets and two or three more are obnoxiously laughing at their intrusions…the rest of them hold excited, sympathetic, courageous, blissful, and other positive expressions. I ensure the complacence of the latter but the former I toss out with my bare fingers, as the golden box moves over to catch them. Those doors shut and the borders of where they open and close disappear, blending back into my skin. I see another with bulged eyes…decidedly dead at my first poke and no bite to follow, so I throw him out as well. The pincher man exits from his compartment in my leg and pinches all doors to my skin closed, returning to his pocket to seal himself tightly from within.

The clear water at my root, still surrounded by those who lifted the door to expose the cups, spills downwards towards my legs and those gathered squeeze a tube attached to me to pump the water upward throughout the full length of both legs. I sit up and stretch my legs, with new found strength in them, and pick up the people to return them to their pockets whose doors still wait open for them. They hold on to my fingers, refusing to let go, and climb on top of one another, stacking up to my head, which is still externally covered with the light yellow green fluid. They press hard into my skin, seeping through the liquid, beyond my scalp, and into the depths of my head. I stand up with a newly cleared head and my legs noticeably stronger.   I start dancing and every part of me is lubricated and gliding smoothly and rhythmically throughout myself.

I see the gold box move slightly from time to time, often entering my dance area. I go to open the box and all of the tiny people it caught lay inside stationary and dead looking. The ones who climbed into my head finish their last dance around my forehead and jump onto the ground at the edge of the gold box. They twirl around holding hands, once this way then the other, and the box polishes into a brighter gold. They stop dancing and jump inside by a similar means of how they reached my head…climbing on top of one another and throwing each other in.

They hand me a dead egg body, all lifting him up together, and place him in my hands. This one I immediately recognize as the one who bit me, and now he wakes, apologetically looking me in the eye, puckering his lips to my finger…sucking the pain out of the bite, soothing it and driving it away. He opens his eyes wider and his body begins to stretch and thin out as he grows into a full sized human who I now dance with. Our fingers interlocked with one hand, our other hands each placed around each other's back, we dance briskly in an orchestrated pattern, moving whimsically throughout our space. I let go of him, rolling him out of my embrace, releasing him to slide across the ice floor into a symphony that has slid in from the ice.

He continues dancing as another from the box, this time a woman who looks more like a fairy than a human, comes to dance with me the same way. The man greets the symphony, who continues to play, and climbs onto their stage which has lowered comfortably into the ice. A man playing a horn stands up and only stops playing long enough to hand his instrument to the dancing man for him to take over. He takes over perfectly and plays for a moderate duration before returning the horn to the horn player and taking on another instrument, a cello next. He gets to experience every instrument, a player from each section amicably offering theirs for him to briefly play.

I dance with the fairy woman for as long as he plays each instrument and as he exits the stage satisfied, I release her from my dance, sliding her across the ice to do the same with the symphony.   The tiny people continue handing me those inside the box until it is empty…each revived participating in a long joyous dance with me, followed by an experience of playing every instrument flawlessly in the ongoing symphony. Each then exits the stage and lays down near the gold box with their backs flat on the cold ice.   They swell up, collecting water around their bodies as the ice beneath them melts.

Once it is emptied, the tiny people jump down from the gold box onto me, running up my chest towards my head, and I wonder how they can run straight up without falling.   Everything becomes pitch black for a second…the box lid closes and opens, and I realize that I am laying down with my back on the bottom of the box with my legs straight up against its wall, and the people are running flat across my chest, not upward…I assumed I had been standing. I see pieces of my head get carried away…out of the gold box into the hands of the small women and men, and I can see with part of my eye on my face that is leaving the box that the pieces are being thrown into the water sacks around the bodies nearby, those who had just finished on the symphony stage.

The water sacks and my head pieces walk over to the box by the will of the people they are attached to. They toss each other high over the edge of the box, back onto my head, reassembling it as it was. I retain the water and the people that came with it drop down my insides, each stopping at a different point within me before settling into stillness to the point I forget them. The tiny men who threw my head parts into the water sacks also climb into my head, holding cups of yellowish green water, and tumble down into my root chakra, motionless from the moment they hit the bottom. I flip out of the box onto my feet and blissfully dance as the symphony continues to play. The dancing and the music continue for hundreds of millions of times of the highest logarithmic expression of the events that happened prior to this. I feel very moist everywhere and I have never danced so smoothly.

6. What the Lights Guard

The red and orange surface I am standing on collapses a bit more every time I shift my weight, but it remains stable enough for me to take a step ahead as I admire the convolutions in its concave nature. I am inside a series of walls represented by a progression of many circles of light within each other, beaming different shades in each ring. Some walls have the dimmest light in the inner most circle, increasing in brightness moving outward, some vice versa…but I notice most have unique patterns of various glow progressions.

There are more than four walls around me but I cannot detect which are surrounding me and which are on the next layer out from the room I am in because the light is translucent and the walls past the walls past the walls are visible for many levels. Depending on the placement of the brightest rings, I can see some things clearly in the rooms besides the walls that enclose them. Most appear relatively empty, but my curiosity is triggered when I see a movement flash briefly in a ring of brightness, rising from an area of the dimmest light…the movement drops again, shielded by the low light.

For the first time since taking a single wavering step on the orange and red spongy surface, I walk forward to investigate. The placement of the walls shifts slightly to adjust to the angle I am facing, so that everything is always forward in relation to my position…there is never anything too far to my sides or at all behind me. I see the movement again as I am drawn closer to the wall to explore its nature and what lies beyond. I feel heat release from the surface of the wall and I assume a living thing tried to cross the wall before my arrival, and is now physically suffering as a result. The ring shaped window of dim light leaves me only a faint outline to study the creature, who reveals only a subtle sway.

I quickly decide I must convey my concern for this being and also investigate further where I am and what else is here. I lift my hand and place my fingertips near the rings of light, choosing to cross through one of medium dimness, balancing my ability to view past it with the amount of heat I must touch, the brighter ones being noticeably hotter. I reach into the light barrier and some great force spits my hand back out to me and it smacks me in the chest. I look down to find a different hand than my own attached to me, one much larger and with more fingers than I had before.

From the place behind me, where nothing is, my lover from another world floats down with his legs crossed and sits down near me with his back turned, and hands me scissors. I cut his long hair, creating a wavy pattern with the ends of his strands and its waves connect his shoulders across his back. He turns around and gives me a gracious smile and without saying a word he drifts off and returns to the void behind me from which he came. With my new hand confidently pushing forward, I cross through the wall that covers the mysterious movement.

I arrive safely on the other side, still with my phantom hand of many fingers. I see the bottom half of a body lay with its stomach facing down, the top half through the next wall on the opposite side of the room I came from, as he slowly inches further into it. The legs and feet look human except there are no toes…the feet are smooth strong flaps, frantically moving. I grab the feet in an effort to pull the body out, but the counterforce is far too strong. I approach the surface of this wall to look deeper in, but there is a magnetic force keeping me from standing closer than a couple feet away. Despite this restriction, I lean over to look as far past the wall as I can. The most ideal bright light, fully exposing the view beyond, is just past the furthest stretch of my height, so I carefully climb onto the back of the body to look in.

This time I am allowed a bit closer than before, and I see a tall stack of colorful jewels that shines in the light that radiates from every direction. Below the stack of jewels, human-like figures with flapped feet like the one I am standing on are piled on top of one another, making up the same distance with their bodies as the height of jewels that sit above them. A small group of elephants lays around this in a circle, embossed with gems and covered with nice carpets and other décor, placed upon them by their masters who sit on top of them…presumably beings similar to the others in the stack, but of a higher order.

I start to wiggle, almost losing my balance, so I jump from the back of the body deciding I had seen enough for now anyway. The room with the jewels and elephants has several rooms leading to it through the passageways of light rings, so I decide to take another way in. This one still repels me with its magnetic force as it sucks the moving being further in.

I use my new hand to reach into the next room, but it again spits it out, leaving the multi-fingered hand intact as my own. I lift it to try once more and it yet again spits me out, this time with a harder smack. In another attempt, I step my foot in first, and quickly fall to my knee but bounce right back up with a new foot, this one larger and equipped with a heavy fur boot covering what was just bare. Stepping in again with my fur boot, I easily access the room that I believe also has a doorway to the room with the action…which has become my destination.

I see a large cube with a long wall going up to the top that I begin to effortlessly climb with the unprecedented traction of my given boot. I instinctively walk up, reaching the top of the cube, and find an old friend from another world sitting with a spiral notebook under a framed picture of her own face that hangs on the wall above her. She holds the notebook and appears to push buttons inside of it instead of writing.   After looking down at this for a while, she shows me her open notebook with a hysterical face acting possessed and excited about the buttons and mechanics of her notebook. She returns again to her natural look and begins writing in the notebook with a pencil as she floats away. I walk backwards down the vertical edge of the cube and stand at the bottom, now seeing light ring beyond light ring, a definite increase from the walls I was able to see prior to climbing the cube.

The next wall appears to lead to the room I am trying to reach, so I attempt to cross this time first with my boot covered foot, which it halfway expectedly

rejects. I chance a second attempt, again to be rejected,

this time diving in head first. I get knocked back with a

hard blow to the head and scrape my back side, sliding

far back into a burning wall behind me. My peripheral

vision has expanded and I place my many fingered hand

onto my face to feel it monstrous sized, with many sharp

teeth. I arrive into the anticipated room and break the

silence with a soft roar that I cannot help constantly

emitting.

I see the men on the glorified elephants stab one

man after other as they break through the walls, trying to

steal the precious jewels. The other beings are much

smaller than my new recently reconstructed body and

easily fly to the sides after each stab, going through the

walls, stuck halfway in and halfway out. I turn and the

walls of light rotate to match my angle as they almost

always do, this time exposing a previously unnoticed

glare between the jewels and the people stacked under it.

I see that the jewels connect to a long blade that goes

through the middle of each body below it. I see the top

body nearest the jewels slowly solidify and turn into a jewel himself, rising above the blade onto the handle of the gigantic sword. This process repeats, and along with each new jewel the pile acquires, one from the line of people dragging on the ground is added to the stack and fixed to the ground, pinned by the sword.

The men on the elephants remove the jewels from time to time and give them to the man that sits on the only standing elephant, who on this occasion leaves to return with good food and precious items for his fellow elite men. Once every few seconds, the pile held together with the sword quickly rotates behind a shield of circular lights, a small round version of the flat walls around us. Somewhere between seeing a selfish smile from one of the elephant men, a wincing glimpse of pain from a man stuck between two walls, and the rotating light around the hefty jewels, I charge into the center, holding my hand of many fingers out and keeping my large head strong and pushed forward. I calculate my landing to be sure my fur covered boot is the first to stomp on the pile when I plow into it. As I am close to reaching it in a mad charge, spears and swords are swung towards me by the men on elephants. I dodge them easily and I kick two of the men far away through the walls, one with each foot. Their respective elephants wreak havoc, knocking down the walls as I approach the center. I am ready to charge into the stack to release the sword and all it holds, and every wall in sight flattens to lay horizontally as they pile on top of one another, crashing onto the top of the highest gem. The mass of rings slams to the ground, collecting the sword, jewels, and fallen ones in its center.

This impact releases the jewels into the air, and they crash down onto either one of the men in the pile under the blade of the sword, or on a man who has just been released by the disappearance of the walls, between which he was stuck. Each jewel that meets a man revives him and he walks away to a place behind me that I still can not see. The rings rise up into the sky with the jeweled sword, illuminating it with a beautiful glow as it turns in the air. The revitalized men drop the jewel after their use for it has passed, and individual rings from the light circles descend, using their natural magnetic force to lift the jewel high onto the handle of the sword…every one thoughtfully placed with a greater luster than it had before.

The men on the elephants rise into the realm of the sword and are swallowed by the rings, disappearing into the light where they will now permanently lie. The elephants stand up and the jewels they wear fall from them onto the back of the largest elephant, who never stopped standing. This large elephant approaches the honored sword in the sky and stands on his hind legs, stretching far to contribute the gems to the handle of the sword. The fine carpets that covered the elephants wipe the blade gently and fall beneath it, catching the sword as it respectfully falls to the ground. The elephants walk away into the void behind me and walking backwards, I follow, finding this is the only way I can move that direction. The walls of light place themselves around the sword, formulating walls to protect it…as they have done before. Not a soul around is in sight…and moving slowly backwards, I admire each shade of light

and the never ending circles on which they shine.

7. Wrong Ticket

I am enjoying a walk barefoot and I reach down to pick a sunflower when suddenly I remember I must check my mail, which is fortunately right below me. With my hands, I dig a small way down to find my copper lockbox, finding it rusty as usual. As I expose the box, the sun rays reach it and the rust falls off into the dirt as I watch the sunflowers rapidly grow. I proceed to unlock the box with a combination of many letters and numbers and once opened, I grab my handful of mail, all tied into tight scrolls. I unravel one after another, finding long messages in languages that I have never seen. I put the scrolls in my bag that dangles low below my waist.

A man rides up to me on his horse with a speedy trot and tells me that I forgot my ticket and I must hurry. I take the ticket from his hand and assuming it is in a different language that I do not know, I do not read it but still know exactly where to go. The day turns to night and I am on an empty street at my destination. A man standing outside tells me that I am too late, but says he can get me through the back entrance. I follow him down the side of a very long windowless building to the back door, which opens downward like a dungeon.

Once inside I see a spiral staircase going up. It is made of glass and there are bodies preserved inside with gel that cycles them around, giving movement to their stagnation. Some have their faces pressed against the cold glass and I feel the chill on my own face. I walk up the staircase, contemplating breaking the glass, but I don't. I walk into a large ballroom, completely crowded except for a perfect circle in the center, taped off with masking tape on the cherry red floor. I stand within it and look high up to the stage and see a puppet show.

The puppets are men and horses and the horses buck the men off unless they can lasso another man from the audience and drop him into the large fish tank adjacent to the stage. Most are getting bucked off as the audience cheers. The ropes are put away and a grapevine drops from the hand of the puppet master. I am suddenly tangled in the vine, rising up above the surprised looking crowd, and I am dropped from a high distance…not falling, but hanging, finding I am one of the puppets.

The men and horses leave the stage and I sit for a moment alone, unsure of what to do besides stare in awe at the huge fireplace at the back of the room…stuffed full of random skulls in its blazing fire. I notice all of the people in the audience are skeletons themselves. My focus on the fire, skulls, and skeletons ceases as women skip onto the stage yodeling. The sound is unpleasant to me, so rather than joining them, I sing a tune of my own. I am jerked up into the air by the grapevine where I hang and face the master, who intimidatingly growls at me and feeds me spoonfuls of seeds that he says I will choke on if I do not chew. I am again dropped to the stage, still receiving spoonful after spoonful as I quickly chew with the yodelers dancing around me.

The audience excitedly claps until they are knocked over by the group that was standing just outside the fireplace, the only ones with skin, as they charge at me with hot shovels that have been roasting in the fire.

They pierce my stomach with them, releasing many seeds which are taken back in the shovels to feed the skulls in the fire. The grapevine catches on fire from the rising flames in my stomach and upon release from the puppeteer, I tumble forward, completely ablaze, and exit the ballroom. I am now a fireball, forward roll after forward roll, unable to find the glass winding staircase. I spill from a gutter into the black open air, and like a comet, I shoot through the sky. My energy dies and I plow into the ground, where I become a pile of ash.

The man who gave me the ticket comes back on his horse, wipes the ash off of me, and I am back in my original form. He steps off his horse, apologizes for giving me the wrong ticket, and hands me another. I put it in my bag with many scrolls and roll down a hill where I know I am meant to go. There I find friendly people and animals playing happily together among trees and bushes covered in many berries. I join them and we laugh, amused by the different colors of berry stains on our skin, and we occasionally partake in the delight of eating one. Once the berries are gone, I give a creature a scroll from my bag and we have story time. After each story we find ourselves with fresh play, as if we had just then arrived to start the fun, and plenty of new berries.

8. How My Heart Once Was

I am tumbling through the air, flipping around in varying directions…I see bees falling with me, every one stinging something. They jump into a honeycomb that falls from the tree that catches me on its biggest branch, and I hang upside down from it by my legs. Near me is a hanging heart…a heart so huge that my current position does not allow a full view. The veins and valves are complex and working together to pump deep through the sky as the heart takes over the clouds, changing the stories in the clouds to follow its pulse, mandating attention to none other.

The clouds disappear with the increasing prominence of the heart and the sky darkens, leaving just enough light to see. The heart rises above our previously shared altitude, and its underside is clear in my outlook. I see a valve open at the very bottom, and from it, creatures made of only heads begin to pour…not falling but floating around, moving only laterally throughout the sky. They frolic in excitement for some time until they stop and face the same direction. The heads drop bodies from them, and they turn from unidentifiable beasts into extraordinarily tall bears.

Tiny detailed groups of veins dangle from the heart, most immediately devoured by the bears…the rest curl up and stick onto the heart, making a sucking motion as if they are drinking from it. The veins multiply and increase in diameter, facing outward to expel blood mixed with balls of fat. The heart quickly drops, falling onto a group of honeycombs that form the surface of the ground. The many holes of the honeycombs hold small plants and little black dots that walk around. Many walking dots, still not identifiable as anything more, stick to the veins as they draw closer to me…the heart is again rising, this time much faster.

Now there is nothing in the sky except a red funnel leading to the top, the aorta of the heart. I am eye height to the gigantic bears who are too busy picking up and putting down honeycombs to notice me. Most take a lick from them, but none seem to like it as they always put it back before the entire portion is finished. The heart has reached a new spot in the sky, this time far above me and the branch from which I am hanging, where it again pauses to rest.

A bear notices me once I take a good long look away from them and towards the heart, and he approaches me abruptly. He reaches to barely touch my hips, to help me off the tree I expect, but before he takes the last step to reach me, he slips and falls on a ball of fat, shrinking and landing inside a honeycomb. Other bears come to clean the fatty blood. They cup high volumes at a time into their large hands before dropping it into my nostrils, giving me a rush of pleasure as it flows down towards my head that hangs below.

The heart gives the sky a gentle shake before turning it into an all-out rumble, sucking all of the bears into the honeycombs, shrinking them at once. The smallest veins drop down like lightning, grasping the contents of the honeycombs, mostly the bears who are no longer recognizable. Just as the veins return to their source, another millisecond after they depart, insects flood the sky as they eject from the heart…one wave of them after another. Like the beast heads the heart first expelled, these creations too, can only move laterally.

They surround the tree above me at the point of the height of the heart and rotate coordinately around it. They freeze still and most fall down around me, a few remaining above in the air. The ones that fall land on various parts of the same tree I am on. The tree evacuates them, evidenced by the sudden fall of every one that lands. The insects still floating in midair slowly lower to the ground level circumference of the tree, then rotate around as they did at the top of the tree.

Their movement detaches this piece of land from the rest, and the base of the tree becomes a honeycomb, floating in a sea of fatty blood that I now realize has been pouring down from my head for a while. The insects that had been evacuated from the tree finally end their slow journey down, landing in the honeycomb holes on the tree island. They come alive and eat the small plants in the honeycomb holes until they are gone and then they jump across the red sea into the long existing honeycombs nearby. As the insects prepare to eat from those, the heart crashes back down, collecting and consuming them into its sticky surface, and springs back into the air…again reaching a different height, this time below me.

This time, no movement takes place in the heart, but every vein and valve that was once inside is now exposed, stretching at its maximum length outward. Heads similar to the first beasts I witnessed, also only laterally mobile, exit the heart smoothly as it sits in a relaxed state. The heads face up from below, looking me in the eye as fatty blood spills from me onto their faces. Human bodies fall from the heads…a few turn human, but many retain the head of a beast. Their bodies develop slowly, starting at the neck progressing downwards. Once their feet touch the ground, each runs to the bottom of the tree with a honeycomb in hand.

As the creatures reach me, they pour the contents into my mouth while plugging my nose. Afterward, they fall onto new empty honeycombs that are rising up from below the ground. The last one to feed me takes me down with him as I experience my long awaited release. I sit with them in the honeycombs for a short time before the heart, with its veins again nicely folded within and around itself, plummets down. Most of its recent round of beings and myself stick to it, and it once more rises high into the air.

It stops abruptly and most of the people fall except for me and a few others, all with human heads and bodies, and we are held back by veins that have readjusted to restrain us. I feel the veins constrict my chest tightly and bees arrive from above, one for each of us held by the heart. A bee lands onto each of our heads and the others fall backwards as they are stung in the forehead, myself spared.

My bee flies away, releasing honeycombs that fall into a tall tower directly below, and then he disappears. I break through the veins with a deep breath and fall atop the tower, landing on my feet. The heart drops to a height just above my head and the tower grows, pushing me up into it. I penetrate the slimy thick texture as I fold into the heart, moving through its chambers, remaining guided by its veins. I feel pulses poke me and I never know which way is up, until I break out of the top to a blue sky with inspiring clouds…

I have a head and feet but my middle is inside of the heart, so I lay down to dream on the clouds of what happened and what is to come. I feel something bumpy and scratchy under my back, so an arm crawls out from the right side of the heart that I use to remove whatever it is. I reach back and grab a small honeycomb the size of my hand and I am inclined to eat it, so I do. At that moment, the remainder of the honeycombs behind me abandon their form to wrap around the heart and turn into me…specifically the skin covering the core of my new body.

I stand up and the sky falls down a few levels, now much closer to me. In awe, I continue to enjoy the beautiful formations in the clouds and a bee flies from them and stings me in the forehead. From this, blood trickles onto my chest, connecting the new skin together like organic glue. The images in the clouds, along with the sky they are in, start to shake. I am aware of this until it connects with the shaking in my chest, where the heart is now safely sheltered, as it intuitively communicates to me. The movements in the sky and my chest never stop, but adjust to one another until they are the same. Then, I walk away in serenity, only stopping to peel a last honeycomb from the bottom of my foot.

9. Lute Bowls

I am treading water not noticing my form, but intently observing the beautiful forms around me. Long graceful water dragons are swimming around occupying most of the space in the sea. None are ferocious or agitated…in fact, they are interacting with one another tenderly. I see one quickly racing along, enjoying her freedom as she emits bright positive lights and vibrations from her opening and closing scales…sharing the emissions with other dragons as they collect them with their own opening scales. I see another twist around playfully, softly tickling the other with the edge of his fin as he passes by, leaving her to smile and confidently turn her head into the nearest bowl of water, floating amongst others in the sea.

The water bowls are wide and shallow and each are the body of a lute, their fret board and long strings pointed high to the sky. Small human-like beings cling to the strings, many with their fingers interlaced around a particular point on the string, remaining immobile with a tight grasp sure not to let go. These stationary beings have unordinary feet, extra long and curved up towards the toe…perfect for the other beings who are the same size and also human-like, except mostly made up of legs. These long legged ones with miniature heads atop jump string to string, as they are flung by the spring of the long feet of their cohabitants who stretch them back and forth as they make lute music. These string leapers occasionally slide up and down the strings…mostly down to land into the shallow water bowl filled with healing water, every creature nearby profoundly attracted to it.

A small number of living things inhabit this bowl, each different from one another but every one has eyes all over its body. They soak in the special water and breathe the rose fog that drifts only in this space, keeping their many eyes on everything around. After observing the living beings around me, I revert my attention to the water dragons who I feel most connected to because of their strong yet playful disposition. Now most all of their colorful scales are open and they are shuffling something around amongst themselves, functioning as if they all share one body in many pieces. Small shiny particles of the dragons release from some of their scales, rising into the air, attaching to a star that then drops down much lower into the sky, almost touching the tops of the lutes.

The night arrives and the water slows down so I can float now rather than tread. I relax and look up to the stars to notice something mysterious hanging down from them. I see the hanging mysteries grow as the long night crawls by and as the sun starts to rise, they take form into developing baby water dragons. I realize my focus has been singly directed towards them all night, and notice my extreme thirst. I dip down to sip water from where I am swimming and see a water dragon close by drink the same water and spin down far below the water not to return, so I spit the water from my mouth. The day passes quickly and with night again coming, I swim toward the water bowl lutes and soon realize the lutes and its occupants are much larger and farther away than I thought.

Floating oil lanterns brush past me and suddenly the water's surface is covered in them. I put my face close to one for warmth and it turns into a cold shadow. From that point, the lanterns all intermittently turn to shadow and back again. Their doing so generates waves in the water that help push me along. I finally reach the group of lutes and pull myself up to peak over the edge of the one I have been most intently observing. I have no hands but instead some sort of loose non-agile extremity that was useful in treading water but now I slip each time I grab for the edge. A red bird lifts me and drops me into the bowl, as I crash into a hard wood floor where I expect to find water. The many eyes on the creatures aboard with me look dry, though from a few, a water trickle drops down here and there, quickly acquired by another beneath it out of desperation.

A rain cloud comes in and I make sounds of excitement which raises the dragons from underwater…until now I had not noticed they were missing. A foursome of long beaked white birds flies in, each holding the corner of a thin white blanket, and stops just beneath the hanging dragon babies, still held by the stars. I hear rain pour heavily onto the surface of the blanket as it collects water and we all look up, anxiously waiting for the water to refill our bowls. With the help of the surface dwellers, I climb the neck of the lute and see that the cloud is extended far away from us. I gather that the purpose of the blanket is to trap water to feed the developing dragons who would not otherwise be able to catch it, which in turn blocks the waters path to our area.

The same red bird that lifted me onto the lute flies up with the rest of his red bird clan in pursuit to pull the blanket aside. The chief bird pokes his beak through the surface of the white blanket where it detaches from him and turns into a large needle about the size of me, I note, as it falls towards me. The needle interlaces into both of my arm-like appendages and lifts me into the air. The needle knits itself into the blanket as I hang from my arm extensions, by the needle that is through the blanket above me. The red birds pull the blanket aside leaving it under the rain cloud, but no longer over the body of water containing the dragons and lute bowls and such. The blanket is still held in place by the white birds on each corner, so the red birds flap their wings, moving the star hooked baby water dragons back to the air space above the blanket. I feel lightweight movement on the blanket above me and feel relieved for the babies who are again able to drink from still water, collected by the white birds and their blanket.

I look down and see water splash up from the area below…it is the raindrops bouncing up and everywhere is refreshed with new water, including the lute bowls which the nature of things so heavily relies on. A massive downpour erodes the thin blanket out of existence, dropping me from the needle's hold with its release. I splash into a filled lute bowl, and drink from it before even looking up to see my exact whereabouts. When I look up I see the many eyes on the few beings next to me are well moistened and slanted upward at the ends, gleaming in joy, perpetually circulating happiness throughout themselves.

I am well nourished and assist the dragons lined up to dip their heads into the shallow lute dish where I sit in the center. The small human resemblances of both varieties come down for a fresh dip. At their return the music moves more fluidly than before and the happiness of everyone is enhanced, detectable by the light rays and sound frequencies bursting out of the glorified auras around us. The air is covered in these vibrations and finally the baby dragons fall down through these layers of energy, into the water where they can now swim and support themselves like the rest of the water dragons.

The stars from which they were hanging fade out and relight, each then moving to the space above a lute. The star unravels the string that the babies were suspended from, and releases it onto the top of its lute, restringing it. Meanwhile, the long legged ones and the large feet string holders join me and the multitude of eyes. The red birds aggressively fly off, pushing away a dark mist of air that begins creeping towards us as the restringing is completed by the energy of the stars. The dark mist's absence immediately allows more sound into the atmosphere that had before been swallowed.

Now with fresh star born strings, watered and revived souls, new water dragons, and my fortunate placement in the bowl, I hear the lute music play proud and strong within the contribution of a mass of energies that unifies us all. In complete peace, I look down to the sea and see that, of course, I was just a baby water dragon not long ago, as I observe my opening and closing colorful scales in the reflection below. I will go jump in the water and play with my friends, I think, as I look up to the head nod of a red bird nearby.

10. Flower Children

I am not sure what I am, but I am something…untouching particles working together in synchronized energy. I am floating around in this demeanor…no colors no odors no thoughts…only natural movements guiding a theoretical me like a choreographed dance…no boundaries or space to bind me…nothing else around except for the orchestrator of my movements. I am not sure what that is, but it is something. A force from the center of my cells, freely rotating through a colorless, spaceless, timeless condition…

Something intrusively spits this motion out of rhythm and I suddenly have awareness from many pieces of this cloud of life energy I have been experiencing. Still amongst the same conditions around me, I see five of my heads spinning around individually as they rotate at a slower pace together in a large circle, moving together much like the simple cells before. This time I can simultaneously see out of all five heads and I feel heat for the first time. I can control the five speeds of individual heads spinning, but there is a minimum speed impossible for me to drop below, which is still very fast.

I focus hard, attempting to concentrate my vision singly from one head to better note the details of the changing space around. I cannot close any of the eyes or slow them down significantly, so I am unable to see where we are, but we are definitely traveling. I develop the ability to move my lips and change my expressions on each face, but that serves no purpose above an annoying distraction. I can sense now that we are going diagonally upwards. The spinning heads turn directions now, counter sun-wise. The darkness falls off like a soft silk sheet from above and the speed of the spinning subsides enough so I can see more of what is around me.

I am now in control of the movement of the five heads as a whole. It is good I have ten eyes and many perspectives to look from because large burning hot balls are now an obstacle. I remember now that I had a single head once, and I lost it by crashing into one of these, so I am cautious to avoid them. In the shape of a downward arc, all five heads swoop down and rise back up, all meeting in the center. In perfect rhythm, this continues repeatedly until we gather around one of the huge hot burning balls. The faces all touch it, burning at first then melting comfortably into it. The individual head spinning aborts as they ease into the average speed suitable for every head's survival, determined by the dominating ball of fire in the center. Our overall speed increases moment after moment until all of the burning balls in sight cataclysmically collapse into the center of the movement.

As they pour into the center with unsurpassable energy, my consciousness feels the balancing force and all of the heads follow me upward, where a flowy gown of silky feminine folds falls from each of our faces…dropping feet and hands from the folds, this becoming our new delicate form. We land tucked to the ground, our heads joined together in the center. The hot ball breaks from below up through the grass which wraps an ice cold dewy layer around the fireball to isolate its heat. It touches the faces and we again stick to it, but this time by frost bite, rather than heat. The heads, still bowing in the center with graceful forms floating out from them, use their new unused hands to keep warm by rubbing them all quickly together.

The small portion of the green coated fire ball surrounded by our heads and hands turns a bright yellow and glows, again generating some heat…this time comfortable. I raise each form from our bow and fall backwards in great pleasure from the fresh air, our feet still connected to the yellow glow in our center. I feel a rush of endorphins and feel my consciousness again go to that timeless, odorless space. I enjoy my ability to see color this time, feeling the motions I intend, and sense an iota of fellow consciousness….

I raise the five bodies from my backwards freefall position, feet still hooked to the middle, and the heat melts us together again. This time I am one, not five. I am now the center. I rotate around my fixed position, relieved at looking through only one perspective, and find five petals around me where the faces were. I am in a flower…no wait…I AM a flower. I sink down into the warmness of myself, shooting down a long narrow stem, gathering the hot thick liquid it contains. In order to hold onto this, my instinct tells me that I need the dark material from the black space below.

I relax all intention and thought, and sink down into the black solid material. The thick hot liquid from my middle flows up and down, its natural way to move, connecting me with the dirt, pushing me into it. Up the stem I go again with a great feeling of hunger fulfilled. Again I have perspective from five faces, seeing each other as flower petals. We rise and hold hands dancing this way and that, and I see more flowers around us, also with five smiling faces…they too, dancing upon their stem. I look up and see some stems are supporting seven or more heads on their dancing bodies, each stem displaying a set of faces identical to one another. I continue dancing until a circle transcending mine, the first one I have seen bearing a variety of faces, comes colliding into us…rotating in and out, one or two of the petal people at a time within my circle, sometimes none until they come back again. As they revisit us, more at a time begin to enter our circle, until finally all of the dancing petal people within this certain stem come into my circle at once. At this instant, they spring into the air, moving incongruently for the first time, not to return. Instead, a soft golden dust falls from the sky in their place. Our circle of petals, from whose faces I can still see, slowly lifts into the air and turns to gold dust.

I enjoy the clear blue sky out of my five perspectives until my vision recedes with each layer of gold dust that begins to dominate my sight. I can feel for a while longer…I experience getting softer and lighter as I display my last expressions on my many faces as they melt into the sky, becoming soft gold dust. I float, I whisper, I go to a place far above until I forget everything. Everything, except, that I am something…I see nothing, I came from nowhere, I do not know where I am headed or if there is anywhere to go. But I know I am some loose form of little dots of bright dust, floating around in a synchronized motion. I see a bright ball slowly approaching as I can sort of begin to see again, though there is nothing to see but this eye-burning hot ball. I expect it to be large because of its heat, but I have no form and see no other forms therefore I have no size to compare it to, no way to define it. Whatever it is, maybe it will have some answers.

11. A Strange Flight

I am learning to fly an airplane being taught to me by a man who slept on the same dark alley as me for several days some time ago…I briefly again experience that time through my memory as I fly through the sky…

I am sitting in the alley lost in memory recall along with a man who normally looks energetic but at this time looks very worn out. We have been looking for the same person who gave us the same odd tasks. After a long joint effort, we cannot find him, so I get going alone…

I run quickly through open windows of identical houses, in a certain order, moving carefully to avoid the traps. There are long thorns trapping the windows, floors with rugs of clothes soaked in acid, a web that needs the strong push of a sharp knife to cut, some rooms filled of toxic gas that seem ok to the naked eye…all thrown at me quickly and I must immediately react exactly the right way to survive, finding the few safe entrances and exits. To effectively avoid these things, I am following my memory of quick instruction communicated by a note that automatically set on fire the instant I read the last word. Until now this has been a subconscious recollection, only now specifically thinking of the note which is presently guiding me on a life-saving detour from the poison waterfall spilling from the door ahead.

I think of the man at the alley, having no idea where he went or what brought him to the same desolate alley as I, but I know he had the same mission as me somehow. I complete the task, ending up on the far west side of the long stretch of hundreds of houses, having successfully avoided all of the traps. Upon reaching the end, where there are no more houses, there is a long rope that gathers to the middle from all around me. Clinging onto it, I spiral downward, lost as to how I arrived here. At the bottom of the rope's lead, I see a man in a dark shadow on the other side of the rope just below me, and I land directly on him. I assume it is he who I have been looking for, so I ask him why I am here. He says he just did the same thing I did and followed me the entire way. He yawns and his mouth opens far up from where we descended, and suddenly the hollow in his yawn shoots up and turns into a rope covered with incremental large teeth, conveniently arranged as perfect steps.

I climb and climb, suddenly arriving in a spacious area, standing next to a flagpole. Beneath me the hollowed out area is outlined by bricks of varying sizes, mainly very large ones. I see a sledgehammer attached to the rope I just climbed that dangles into the open arena below. The bricks comprise the walls and floors of the whole surface area and there is no one else around. An aroma of burnt hair saturates the air. I swing the sledgehammer like a pendulum, back and forth, as it drives far to the walls by the glide of the rope. I am swinging as fast and hard as I can, repeatedly aiming for the same targeted chunks since each collision merely chips away at the wall that I focus on breaking through. After fifty swings or so, two holes develop in the walls facing each other on either side of me, cumulatively impacted by every hammer blow. I hurriedly jump a long way down and out through one hole I just made, to find myself in a similar space, this time with no sledgehammer.

I reverse my steps back to where I came from, grab the sledgehammer, and return to my safe original escape route, briefly stopping to contemplate exiting through the other hole I made, but this option is quickly eliminated due to the hole having already reclosed enough to block me. With the sledgehammer, I again climb up to a high hill in the new space, and swing the hammer again and again. I break through and find myself doing the entire process a third time, this time sure to bring the sledgehammer.

The old friend of mine, from the alley, wakes up from a secluded corner in the final room, yawning out of the mortar between the bricks. From the mortar, his mouth develops and he sleepily mutters that he has now slept the longest sleep he has ever slept, and he can't understand why he got so lost the day we met and that he only followed me on the task because he got the instructions delivered to him, wrapped in hair, after the paper burnt and now he is here to fly me out. He jumps into the hole opening that I made with the abrasive pendulum swings as he grabs my hand and pulls me into the airplane. Again he yawns and says he hadn't been conditioned for all that rope climbing as he jumps inside of my mouth. I feel his snore like a purr.

I lift away in the airplane with ease and feel a huge urge to fall asleep. I wake up and I am tossing a paper airplane I made into the air, blowing it for extra flight force. It goes far and as it flies away, I see words written on it, so I chase after it, running faster and faster until I am running alongside a real airplane that is taking off into the air. I am again blowing the paper airplane, keeping it in flight, as I run beneath the other airplane while it climbs higher and higher. The paper airplane begins to simultaneously fall slowly down with the other, and the air gets noisy all around as they both draw near. I catch the paper airplane to reveal the message disclosing my next task, escorting me to peace. As I turn around to set foot on this mission, the other airplane ceases its fall and again climbs to its journey across the sky.

I, of course, am operating it…

My memory is clearer than ever and my capacity for learning is high…

12. Skin Trip

I am taking a bath enjoying the weightlessness of my head as it floats on the water…my stomach pushes my body up and down, I am breathing deeply in and out as I slither on the water's surface. I push my entire face down underwater, holding my breath, and the water splashes up with force as if the tub turned upside down and it comes crashing back down past the tub below me, leaving me in the dry bathtub.

The water lands inside in a deep crystal beneath the surface, which I can see through the reflection of a shard of glass that I catch after it drops down to me from above. In the reflection, a small ball sprouts directly up into the tub, growing below me and around me, and finally through me where a cactus rises from me. My veins break, splitting in half and rooting onto the sides of the tub as they tie together like yarn…arranging themselves into a supporting cradle for my brains to fall into, the rest of my interior following.

The cactus continues to grow, rising through the air, grabbing remnants of my skin as it ascends. Enough of me goes up that the pieces recognize each other and regroup, again resembling their original shapes into the form of my skin…it climbs up with the cactus, ultimately reaching a destination on a layer of sand above. The parts of my brain unwind into a large strand, outlining the edge of the tub in many layers, as my eyesight shifts perspective into its elongating entirety. I see my insides first cling together, shriveling in response to the cold surface of the steel tub, then separate, releasing the immense heat from the overbearing flames that come up further every moment from just beneath. This explains the burning smoky smell on the cactus that my dangling nose detects. Shifting and stirring in the tub, my insides find their perfect comfort, with the exact placement of every piece, conducted by the tub.

Meanwhile, my eyeball-less sockets can see a flickering glance of sight out of the mass of skin on which they sit, and I detect a desert densely covered with only cacti. I myself dangle from one, as my skin hangs like a blob of chewed debris enmeshed in cobwebs, its allotted time there far expired. The air lays still and all I can do is hang there in my skin, or, relay my consciousness to my basking insides on the icy hot steel tub below. Above, a trail of bugs approaches and shows me how to hold my head to direct the wind and to which way it should be directed in order to push me where I want to go, which they also determine for me, thankfully, for I am at a loss.

My chin treading heavy, I force it upwards into the air, with my empty neck stretched far back. The wind erupts and the cactus releases me into the air, where another postpones my progression, capturing me in its pins. I redirect my head as instructed by the bugs, to the forward and right of where I am now caught. Again succeeding, I am released and land on another cactus. Here I spot the hole in the ground within the group of four cacti around it, just adjacent to me, as prophesized by the bug trail. Rodents climb from the hole, and run far away just out of my sight until their footsteps end with the sound of a splash. I wait patiently until the hole completely empties, then I fall in by the force of the wind that I easily seem to beckon.

My skin falls onto my newly constructed interior and I am placed on a green leafy seat with small flower vines around it, sitting in the steel tub. I jump up and feel like I am moving much faster than I could have ever imagined, and take off running into the far distance, the fresh air soothing me and removing the cactus thorns as I quickly recover.

13. The History of Leprechauns

I go to a long narrow hallway to listen to a history lesson conducted by a man who has lived for many centuries. He speaks slowly, so slow that it sounds like he is making droning sounds rather than speaking with words. He is at a podium with a large book open, looking the crowd in the eye and not down at his book, but turning the pages as if he is reading from it. He slams the book shut and says none of it matters anyway and we can all go home now. I am at the back of many motionless heads that remain still at the time of the lecture's dismissal. I stand up and walk out, unsure of where I am to go. I feel like I have never left this place but I am glad to be out now in the fresh air and sunshine. My feet are stuck to the ground and I walk with a scoot to progress.

I come to a lake with chunks of floating clay, so I sit next to it and start making pottery…first, a jug so I can drink. The water I drink pours through me and out through the gaps between my toes and now I can pick up my feet and walk properly. A lumberjack near me says I will never get anywhere without my clay jug, and hands me what I made which I had forgotten by the water. Even though he hands it to me, I walk back to be sure I didn't forget anything else.

I go back, not too far from where I had just been, and there is a long narrow building above the lake where I am now standing. I enter and the same man is speaking the same way, still of history, but he is explaining the collapse of the big hallway that we were in before and is instructing us to all look for the vandal as he describes their appearance. He says the person has no skin on half of their face.

I step outside where there is a funeral procession with tambourines playing in abundance. Disturbed by the miserable faces, I go back inside and as I grab the door handle, the lecturer spins nonchalantly from the doorway, as if taking a break, and pushes me against the wall with bulging eyes looking into mine. "You've got to get out of here NOW," he insists, "the other students will be turning around to leave soon, and no one can see you." He returns to the building's interior, shutting the door behind him.

Leprechauns are painting the outside of the door which distracts me until I see something slide out from under it. I reach down, pick it up, and see my image in the face of a small mirror. My face is only half covered in skin and my reaction is to scream. I scream and a thick coagulation of dark red blood spills onto the surface of the mirror displaying the words, "It's not your fault." The mirror drops from my hands and one of the leprechaun men picks it up with all of his might and places in on the tips of my toes. Nails drop from the mirror, piercing my feet, fixing them to the ground, and I do not bleed…but the blood expelled from my mouth gathers along the wound as if it had come from there.

The students look out from the window and start cheering. The leprechauns laugh and mock human celebration as they twirl rapidly in circles, linking arms and grabbing each other's hands. They take turns pinning each other to the door to accent their art piece, and each one drops their internal liquid of different colors down the surface of the door. After the pinned ones hang for a few moments, they cooperatively assist each other in undoing their pinned friends. They then fall and laugh, unbothered and physically undamaged from the apparently painful scenario.

A few new ones crawl up from a hole in the ground and approach me, together working with all their strength to pull the nails from my pierced feet. They tell me it's easy to bounce back from sharp incisions like that, as long as I use my bodily fluids as art on the door, because each of us has a completely unique color. I wipe my freshly released foot blood onto the door, contributing my own color. The door falls as if bearing too much weight, and the leprechauns are all covered by the fallen door. I hurry to pick it up, racing against the stampede of terrified humans scurrying to the same door for exit. I make it in time to lift the door, finding all of the leprechauns with skin on only half of their faces, each crying a different color, exposing the bloody inside of their faces that matches their tears. A lake forms beneath us and their fluids harden into clay.

I use this clay to make a jug and fill it with water from the newly formed lake, and gently pour the water onto each one of them. They slowly reanimate and crouch down around me, hiding from the masses of people still running from the building. To ensure they are safe in their hiding, I do not move, and during this time, the skin on their faces gradually grows back. I lay back relieved of their revival, tilting my head up, and see a lumberjack chopping down the building. He is different than the other one, but looks over and winks at me before returning back to work.

The leprechauns climb onto my head and work their hands in a delicate motion, rubbing their saliva onto my face. I feel my skin tighten and I feel strong. I sit up, confident in my friendship with the leprechauns, and carry them back to the door where they were painting, which still lies on the ground without the building it was once attached to. They climb under it, pulling me with them, and I fall into a peaceful sleep as they tell me stories of their hobbies, families, and beliefs, to which I perfectly relate.

I wake and only one is still there with me. Together from beneath the door, we lift it up and find ourselves in a long narrow building. He runs up to the front and I walk towards the back, following my inclination of where the door has been placed after suddenly going missing. I find the door, walk outside, take a sip from my jug, and return inside to find a lecturer speaking to an intently listening crowd. I sit quietly in the back and listen to the beginning of a fascinating tale of where the first leprechaun was found and how he discovered his mate. A few sentences in, the people leave looking frustrated, talking amongst themselves of how they could not understand the lecturer. One kicks over my water jug and it spills onto all their feet as they collapse to the ground, pinned into the dirt, wincing in pain. I dump the remaining water on them, and they each turn into several tiny leprechauns.

The lecturer comes to me and says it's not my fault and he hates to sound selfish, but he needs a few more doors anyway. He tells me that he needs me to write an account of all that has occurred today, because he is late to teach his history class.

14. Snakes & Petunias

I am on the arc of a wheel up high, receiving filled buckets of water from above me…I throw my hands up to catch them and I pour the water out, where it automatically tips from bucket to bucket below me until it ends up in what from here looks like a large well in a larger body of water. It is surrounded by large green patches of lily pads and drifting moss and other grasses, growing right from the water. With each bucket I empty, I move a position closer to the well by tumbling into the next space affixed to the wheel behind me that is turning towards the ground. As I move into the spaces nearer to the bottom, I rock more intensively each time…evidently preparing to tip into the water, separated from the rest of the ocean around us by the sturdy brick circular well, built high and nestled within the bountiful green life that rises throughout the waters.

As I approach the bottom of the wheel, my rocking maximizes as I swing backwards and see big tree frogs licking sap from a ceiling where their feet are attached. A different type of sap with a thinner consistency drops from the backs of the frogs into the buckets. My body swings forward with the natural cycling of the wheel, turning my vision from the ceiling clinging sap frogs to the last space I am tumbling into before I reach the well. I land in the last hanging space, comforted by the thickness of the pour that I know now is tree frog sap, and I watch its prior contents drop into the brick circle as I gaze on the lily pads and moss piles everywhere around it…wondering if I can see out once I drop in.

Before I know it, a bucketful pours onto me, tipping my space over as I fall out onto a path that seems to have come out of nowhere. A man and woman wearing identical clothes of wrapped vines say to me at the exact same time, "These are petunias…" while each holding one hand out as if offering something and pushing it through the air with their palms up as they draw a landscape of pink petunias around them, now encompassing my entire view. Some of the flowers fall into my hands, forming a nice bouquet. I give it to the lady and she hands it to her mate, doubling the bouquet, as she still holds the original. They both take single flowers from it and place them on the ground where they turn into silent people who are laughing. The laughing people are pleasant and soft and make no noise but exude much peace and comfort. They come close to me, reaching my hands, and turn into a bouquet of flowers placed within them.

    The couple and I fall through the path, travelling through a layer of lily pads, and land inside of the brick well. I whip my head out of the water for air and a snake comes to me and puts the end of his tail inside of my mouth, sliding into me backwards. Before completely going inside, he sways his tongue around a few times out of my mouth, briefly gaining control of my face. He drops down into me and many other snakes follow the same way, and I again fully submerge underwater. The woman and the man each take one of my hands, the woman on my left and the man on my right, and at the same time they speak into my ears, "They just don't want to have poison anymore." The snakes are inside of me from head to tail and I feel the top head occasionally come out of my mouth to flip his tongue quickly through the water from my lips. The pair, still holding my hands, use their outside free hands to swim us up to the surface. They thrust me into the air and push my feet up with their hands. They turn me upside down and the frogs drop down from long strands of sap and pull the snakes out of me, one by one, throwing them outside of the brick border, most stopping to rest on a lily pad before they jump into the sea.

The man and woman pull me back into the water inside the well and we swim down using both of our own hands independently until we reach the bottom. The woman and man offer their hands out and move them together across the air, again bringing a forest of petunias around us. We sit down in a line, the man in the back, then the woman, and me in front. The man leans backwards to draw water from the well behind, while the woman holds his feet and I hold hers. He passes the drawn water up to her, then her to me, and I pour it in every direction to water the entire area as it grows thick with fields of petunias. We do this many times and we see other various blossoms arise as we keep watering.

A snake comes from my mouth and projects far ahead pouring his venom onto the flowers everywhere around us, dispensing far more of his liquid than we had fresh water. Silent people emerge from the flower bunches, smiling and laughing, still softly and elegantly and pleasant yet remaining completely silent. The snake withdraws from the gardens back into my mouth and the flowers grow at an escalated rate. The three of us continue the watering process, elated the entire time. The snake within me is pacified and holds no poison, filled only with life-giving waters to dispense everywhere. Our presence is often graced by the visit of frogs hopping on the lily pads nearby, replenishing everything with fresh sap. As this occurs, the hillside shifts slightly to embrace the most pleasant view.

15. Cloud Dwellers

I am sitting on a deep chair made of canvas, dragging along…pulled by the means of an unseen force over a bridge with nothing below it, only infinite space. Dry crumbled half burned pieces of paper cover its surface, and all is silent except for the crunching of the charred paper below. My speed increases as the piles of pages grow larger, and another sound joins the solitary crumbling. I hear popping snaps of bubbling liquid and my chair ride on the bridge takes a sharp turn up a steep incline to the right, towards the sounds, into the shadows. The canvas on my chair drops from its frame, stretching almost to a break, and cups me close to the ground as I continue on the path, unable to stand up or separate from my chair. This allows me to study the atmosphere and I see clusters of lava meander throughout tiny tributaries along the canyon above. These increase as I move forward and the area lights up so much that I must squint…although despite the lava drizzles, I know I am deep in the dark.

I look up and see a cave building up around me, formulating before my eyes by the power of the hot lava. My chair vessel now guides me downwards, and the lava's brightness is left to saturate the space overhead, a beautiful glow from above like a candle glazed chandelier.   Also above I see layers of protruding ground, like balconies, placed every few yards, holding stone statues captured in odd positions…chillingly lifelike, caught in surprise, as if the faces are frozen on that exact moment when joy turns to misery…some with faster reactions than others…a man stuck halfway between sitting down and standing up with an unflattering expression accompanied by a dropped jaw and weary eyes…a woman sort of looking at me but with a slight eye cross and one side of her lip dropped down low as she stands tilted forward and uneasy...the rest, similarly off guard.

I try to stand but my legs will not straighten. The ride gets bumpier and the chair tries to eject me at full speed but I hold my hands tight around the arms and stay on.   I exit the cave through an unexpected doorway and my chair transforms into a long wooden canoe, both ends rising to a point. It tips nose first and I drop several feet down from the cave's exit into a never ending ocean of flowing lava. The stone statues, all twenty or so of them I saw in the cave, crash down into the lava close behind, and papers float from their hands into the air, blowing towards me as they fall. I grab the papers from the new wind and place them in the covered front lip of my canoe. I tuck my head under to block the wind in order to read them, but I find they are undecipherable with smeared lines of illegible ink across them. I keep them in a safe place, secured behind a vertical piece of wood under the front of the canoe.

The sound goes silent again until I hear sporadic splashes. I look to see the fallen statues swimming towards me through the hot lava. They start jumping aboard, looking straight past me to the notes…one after the other they climb on as I move to the front of the boat to grab the papers. As they keep piling on, the canoe wobbles more and more and suddenly we capsize. They instantly turn back to stone as I am swallowed into the lava, unable to recover the canoe. I smile as I feel my skin reveal its last sensation to me. I float upward, viewing the lava land below, yet I feel like I am falling far far down.

After a long fall I land in a canvas chair, this one wrapped in feathers and beads with a foot pedal attached to a low bass drum. I tap my foot to sound the drum and a small pool of lava drops from a huge rock shelf above. It bubbles and pops loudly and I see lips moving inside, further developing into form, singing a chant that proceeds their image. "Ha-yah-yay-eh, ay-yo-yay-yah, hey-ha-yah-yay, eh-ya-yo-yah, yo-yah-yay…" They chant this precisely as they back away from the lava, developing into full grown bodies attached to umbilical cords. Their size is close to mine, but all other appearance is hidden from me, their bodies covered head to toe in thick dark mud and long feathers. All ten or so of them step back from the lava, and turn to their right to stomp on their brother's umbilical cord, breaking it. The cords snap into the air like a quick whip and recoil back into the lava.

The brothers continue their "Ha-yah-yay-eh…" chant and push the lava down using a graceful hand motion, and pull me and the canvas chair I am on into the middle. They chant louder as four of them come near me each kicking down a side of my chair, the others waiting to greet me after catapulting high into the air from my chair's release. They ask where I came from, and as I open my mouth to explain, they bombard me with mud and feathers. This requires much adjustment for me to move and leaves me with no ability to speak…but these effects quickly disappear as I familiarize my new form and push the mud from my mouth with my tongue. We lay down to sleep, each wrapped in our own large roll of canvas that has expanded from the fabric of the chair.

We wake to the canoe dropping from the sky as it crashes into the dry ground before us. We climb in, seated in a long row, and chant as I remember the notes I hid in the front which is in arm's reach. I grab for them, finding even more than there were before, along with a hammer and nails. Us muddy feathered ones hop from the canoe and line the notes across its floor surface to observe them. I interpret the smeared ink entirely differently this time, though it looks exactly the same…I now see them as patterns. We pass the hammer up and down the line of us, each pounding the nails into the canoe, following the pattern on the notes. The nails vanish, leaving only a hole after they are pounded through. Lava pours from above, forming a pool as before but this time it keeps filling and filling, higher and higher…spilling over our feet and still rising. It burns badly but it is just bearable, thanks to the protection of the mud and feathers. We complete the note pounding, the canoe now raised to our shoulders, floating higher with the rising lava. Just before the lava consumes us, a draw bridge drops down with large complex pulleys and hooks on its end, approaching us. The holes we hammered into the canoe fit the hooks perfectly and as we climb the steep grade bridge, back in the canoe, the pulleys and hooks effortlessly elevate us away from the rising lava.

We reach the top far, far away…rising up until we look down at the endless sea of lava that now appears as a single microscopic drop of red in a white background. We sit in the canoe and chant for many days. Day by day the canoe gradually changes to canvas. We eventually stop chanting and find ourselves in never ending blankets of canvas with the most comfortable seats and beds around us that we could ever ask for. I stop, having obtained true clarity from my days of chanting, and smile with an epiphany that the canvas is my cloud…one of the many clouds in the space I live. I hop to another cloud nearby, loving my home, as I wave goodbye to my neighbors, the chanters, for now…

16. Life of Flies

I bend over to pick up a small creature apparently suffering on the ground. I enclose the frog-alligatoresque being in my palm for a moment to warm him. I feel my fingers become sticky and in order to not bind myself together, I unfold my hand. From here, time changes and all events move at twenty times or so the speed I am used to. Upon extending my fingers open from my palm, the creature now has a mate. At the highest speed my eyes could possibly follow, the amphibious creature mates with his partner and produces enough offspring to fill my entire palm. With my left empty hand, I reach to grab a fly to feed one that is obviously desperate for food. The baby creature, being of the others and trekking on intense speed intervals, quickly jumps into my left hand to claim his feast. He too, summons a mate to join him in my hand, and they too mate, bearing many offspring.

My hands grow as their population grows, prompted by the feeling of the sticky residue their tiny feet leave on my hands. After I acknowledge the second set of offspring, the ground shakes, creating huge cracks in the land around us, from which an enormous alligatoresque beast emerges, standing much taller than I, a ways ahead of me. He yells, "GOOOOOOOO," as the vocal chords visually rattle in the back of his mouth like plucked strings. The beings residing in my hands look towards the large beast with their red eyes and each makes a sound of their own in response to him, in an attitude of fear and obedience. The noises are loud and projected with different volumes and tones, none at all the same which sounds chaotic and creates constant unease in the environment.

The families in my palms have quickly grown dependent on me, so I take great measure to not disturb them, despite the noises that are painful for my ears to take in and are stressful and displeasing for the brain to decipher. "GOOOOOOO," from the large beast is still the master sound in the air, until large flies come from his mouth in high abundance…some squeezing through the gaps of his large fangs on the frontline of his deadly clenching jaw, others exiting smoothly from his mouth opening, and some charging out with higher momentum than the others by pushing off from his tongue. The swarm is making a high pitched sound, like an over amplified version of the normally unnoticeable sound of a light bulb or electricity. The beast's flies swarm past me and the creatures on me watch them with longing in their eyes which are turning black. It is obvious they are hungry for them, but the beast sees this and stops releasing so many flies. A human rolls from his tongue, expelled onto the ground with the force of the beast's growl which he sounds simultaneously with his ongoing "GOOOOO" yell. The "OOOO" comes heavier as time passes.

The beast, who is rooted into the ground, sways in all directions with his top half, mostly comprised of his head, in as much chaos as the noisy sounds that are ruling all of my senses. In the visual scope of his wide open mouth I see dead flies stuck between his teeth, in the back of his throat, and along his gum line…rotating in these positions as they float around his mouth like a river. As it becomes difficult for his sounds to break through the presence of the dead flies, he spits them out onto the human freshly fallen from his tongue, and the man instantly dies. I carefully bend my knees down, keeping my palms straight up to keep the life in my hands pacified, and move my fingers toward the dead man's body. His eyeballs are missing and the sockets are now a warm spot for baby maggots. My sticky fingers are able to collect the flies and maggots by contact, so I touch my fingertips to each one and feed my hungry critters.

The large beast swings around more frantically than ever with less sense of rhythm than before and his sound rises many decibels. A freefall of flies pours from his mouth like a fountain, as heaping amounts fall down in a single fluid gush. Keeping my palms faced up, I alternate moving each arm foreword with the force of my elbows as quickly as I can to catch the flies. My intentions are clouded and I can hardly decipher my thoughts or actions as the yelling and shrieking, always increasing in volume and varying its pitch, infiltrate my entire consciousness. Words are spoken in the yells but I can't make them out. I am, however, happy that I have a focus…feeding the needy creatures on my palms. I catch flies as quickly as I can and the fountain of flies falling from the beast begins to thin. Within this opening, I see eyes on the tongue peeking out from behind the curtain of flies. I wait for the beast to whip around with his mouth open towards me again, and I work even harder to clear the flies to get a better look. Fingers then grasp the empty space, flustering for survival, and I see the eyes and fingers belong to a terrified human.

I am more synchronized with the creatures moving twenty times my normal speed, now able to adapt to this pace myself. After the clearance of the flies, the suffering man slides out onto the ground, coughing out foreign material which he proceeds to sort out and put in tubes, marking them with three red xs. I continue to clear flies with my sticky fingers, feeding them to my vocal minions, as the visual details of inside the beast's mouth are further revealed. Another human is exposed, grasping onto the beast's tonsils and other fleshy parts, struggling for survival as he flails his arms everywhere in constant slips and falls. A similar escape is attempted by many other men, and only two or three of them make it out who are too, covered with flies, eye sockets emptied and filled with baby maggots. I try to save them all, but unfortunately the combination of compounding noises, the nurturing of the palm creatures, and my new adaptation of functioning at twenty times my usual speed, makes the task impossible most of the time.

A person washes up from the depths of the beast who treated me badly in the past, giving me injuries I can still feel. For the first time during this encounter, I go past my automatic actions, contemplating the situation and what the "right" thing to do would be. I settle back into my normal speed and grab the flies at a natural pace, neither sitting still nor rushing, to keep his fate balanced without my pull in either direction contributing to it. The most desperate and persistent of all, this one keeps swimming up the tongue, terrified and in obvious pain, as I try to minimalize my involvement in the rather personal piece of the situation. He wails in pain and surrenders his attempts, as the beast sucks him back inside. One more washes up after him and this one is saved as I clear his exit, once again moving at super speed, feeding my dependents the last of the flies that the beast's mouth provides…and all the sounds stop.

I look down to my palms and my fingers have stretched to great lengths and there must be thousands now living on my hands. The beast turns around and bites my hands off, ingesting them along with the thousands of froggish creatures and all the flies in their bellies. Reacting to the pain, I push my wrists into the dirt for relief, right where the first suffering creature was found. New hands are now growing from my wrists, the normal size I remember from long ago, but maybe this time a little stronger.

17. Blood Red Moon

I am standing moon gazing at the red full moon. Half of its surface area collapses to the center and a large claw pointing down protrudes from it. The pores of the moon contract as if pushing the claw away from it. Hypnotized, I watch the claw spin round and round as it quickly gains speed before stopping once again, this time with its point facing upward. In a smooth motion it is expelled from the moon at a great speed, and with its tip still facing upwards, it pierces the tenderest part of my throat, hooking into it. I get an instant adrenaline rush of ecstasy and let out a high pitched note which resonates with the air around me and in it, I suddenly hear many such sounds.

I make this sound for a long time and as the claw guides me to the sky, I travel facing directly upward. I squeeze into one of the tiny pores of the moon as it continues to contract. The noise I make stops and as it does, I see the sound waves turn to waves of high energy that saturate the moon. I am now fully inside and I have a thin layer of wet sticky material around me. The pulsing and contractions move me around in my sticky sack and it feels like someone else is picking up the bag and slamming it down repeatedly. The sack breaks and my head comes out and I see other beings in the same sacks around me, also with their heads breaking out from them. Our heads shake rapidly, our bodies still in the sticky bags, convulsing behind our heads. The shaking becomes so fast I feel I may explode, but I am thankful I have a bag to catch me if I do.

The energy level is approaching what seems like more than I can take and my head drops to my stomach as I fall thousands of times faster than the pull of gravity…I am out of the sticky bag…cut vertically down my center by a lightning bolt, which induced my fall. I look a long way down and see the tiny vision of a distant Earth. I look up as the moon jumps towards me and away again while I dance through the air in my lightning bolt's control. I am one of eight other beings undergoing the same experience as we fly through the sky on our bolts, occasionally overlapping one another, all connected at the top…at the red moon, now turning into a face.

The moon face is controlling the bolts that we are attached to as her eight legs. I desperately want to talk to the face but she cannot hear me. I rip the front vertical axis of my skin as I tug myself forcefully backward, releasing myself from the bolt. I fall and it gets unbearably cold fast, so I hang onto the bolt, the leg of the moon woman, from the outside, hugging it with my shoulders tight and my wrists crossed behind it. The cut down my center binds to the bolt as they meld together, and I now can comfortably let go. The lightning sucks back up to its source, its life head, and I am again in the moon. This time I can see out of her eyes and I release the other seven people and their bolts back to Earth, as they beg me to do. The void where the lightning powered beings were has been filled with rubbery legs that I can feel and control. I play in the freedom and move them around elegantly. I enjoy my smooth, hairless form that allows me to cut gracefully through the sky, and I am thankful for whatever is allowing it to happen and I don't want it to end.

I am suddenly hungry, finding myself in a bubbly sea filled with long slender fish. I open my mouth to eat one, but instead of going inside of me, his lips outline mine. My lips curl back and pull tight over my face like saran wrap, and suddenly I am suffocating. I am happy when I get the sensation of soft pain, ensuring me that I am alive, and tiny thorns are poking me everywhere. The membrane of my stretched lips pops and I can breathe again. I am now shuffled around with many other items the same size as me, and we are dumped out of a giant scoop onto a giant sphere from which everything else falls off…but I remain at the exact top of the sphere, now recognizing it as a crystal ball. I touch myself to see what form I am in, and I am human, but it seems so unfamiliar.

I relax, laying my tummy down on the crystal ball, and look down. I see a center split diagonally in two on a flat plane at the bottom, with a zebra and a leopard pressing their foreheads together. I drop food to the animals, finding a surplus in my hands, but it takes a very long time to get there. When it does, the animals oddly don't notice and their heads are unwilling to part. Tiny animals run from the far perimeters of the sphere into the center and eat all of the food. It turns out to be poisonous and they collapse. The two animals look up to me and I am surprised they can see so far. A human parts the animals and begins to write a letter, the content of which the animals are relaying to him. The man turns into an insect and flies to the top of the crystal, out of it, into my nostril, and drops the note into my heart, where it is translated to me in indescribable depths. I am touched, for the message is beautiful.

I can suddenly see much more detail and there are many planes in the crystal ball, beyond the single plane on the bottom that I first observed. I remove the item of clothing I am wearing and with it, I sand the top of the crystal profusely. There is a small space within the planes of the sphere that I fall into, and I am stuck, but deeply touched by the piano playing on the plane diagonal to and slightly below my space. I am so touched by the music that I cry, but I am perfectly content. I see all of the planes around me through the translucent crystal and people throughout the layers are hugging. The music gets stronger and I stop crying, wondering why I am all wet. The liquid leaks everywhere, cleaning the intermittent solid space of the walls and the exterior of the crystal ball. The people are still hugging and they start crying, bathing one another with their tears. Everything is so clean and full of love right now, and oh the piano is oh so beautiful that the silence afterwards hurts. The silence surrenders again to the perfect sound of the music and I don't remember the music ever stopping again.

I am still in my closed space, and for the first time everyone notices me at the same time. They knock on my floor from below, and I motion for them to hush and enjoy the song. They further attend to their tears, participating in cleansings of all sorts with their drops. I again sand the top of the crystal with my clothes, and climb out from within. After holding my breath for quite some time, I drop my eight legs around the crystal ball and project it high into the sky…and from afar, I admire the moon.

18. Mask Infusion

Tumbling through a long polished wooden chute, I am released and set into motion with a series of summersaults. I sit up, dusting the dried leaves from my face, and breathe hard, eliminating the debris from my lungs. A gathering of children crowds around a cage, what is in it, I cannot see due to the excited children laughing and jumping around it. I ignore them and walk up a short hill just beyond. At the top of the small slope, a few steps lead up into what looks like nowhere. I peak around the side of the steps and see men with long beards and long hair squatted down, swinging their bent knees out and back together again, moving their hands and arms like they are grabbing and climbing…repeating this in the form of dance. They wear masks that cover only their head and eyes, every one different and rich in design…beastly, exotic, and alive. I stop for a short look, quickly retracting my head behind the steps to remain unseen. The edge of my face peeks from the other side of the steps, allowing the corner of my eye a glance. I see the same thing on this side, completing most of the picture as two rows of men wearing masks, facing each other, participating in this dance…freely but together, sharing the same movements yet all in their own time…all wearing masks of intense beasts, staring high into the middle.

I slowly crawl up the steps, keeping my head low to prevent being seen from the top step. I look back to be sure the kids are still distracted, and they are…but with what I still don't know. I cautiously stretch my neck to look over the top step, and I am suddenly in a long line of people on the steps. Everyone else is in front of me and as I realize I am in line, they turn to look at me. They are wearing full extravagant masks that cover their entire faces…far more complex than the half masks of the men dancing by the stairs, although both kinds are stunningly animated and alive. Most masks in line with me hold extra attributes like beaks, fangs, large protruding jaws that change their entire head shape, or horns of various types. They stare at me for a moment and the one closest to me sweeps me up with his tusks and throws me over the edge. I land at the feet of the row of men to the right and they dance, stepping over me and back again, and for the first time, they stop. They slide over a long narrow crate filled with masks, many made to wear down to the shoulders or even further down. I don't choose but I pick one up without deciding…one with a long deep narrow jaw and two long straight horns with needle sharp points, and stripes that cover down to a furry chest. The slender tongue sticks out and is curled up to the inside corners of the sternly expressed prominent eyebrows.

I am back in line with the other masked people, now behind and in front of me. We individually climb to the top step, leaving the others behind blind to what happens at the top. My turn comes and dressed in my mask, I step up. Two massive logs stretch straight out ahead above me, with shorter logs loosely placed horizontally across them. The two rows of half masked men below have resumed their dancing, and I see what I am here to do…climb across the platform to the beautiful branch entanglement ahead…the most perfect looking, comforting space…a whirlwind softly spinning in grace…its branches call me to come into its center, pulling me in with its lively fingerlike motions, and I want nothing else…

I jump off the ledge and grab the first small log, my hands above holding tight as I hang, ready to leap to the next. Dangling, I see the newly visible sight below that was before blocked by the cliff from where I jumped…a forest of dried yucca and jagged rocks, outlined with needles and pointy sticks and topped with assortments of tree cones. With his tiny sharp claws, a squirrel scurries over my hands bouncing log to log, and smoothly sneaks one of them away as he runs with it out of sight. This makes for a difficult leap ahead, so I get going…taking this as a hint of urgency. I let one arm go, holding the other tight, and swing to the second log. The foot taps of the dancing men below make a subtle beat on the earth, like a quiet drum on my heart as it thumps. The third log is the last one before the gap with the missing log from the squirrel's visit…so I breathe deep and push my arm through the air, reaching for the next log, to complete my last small jump in the first cluster. As I grasp it with my left hand, the log turns towards me and I slip from its surface, towards the fearsome jagged wilderness that awaits beneath. I rotate through the air, twisting my body toward the ground, and land upside down, cradled by the sharp points of the long horns on the top of my mask. The level of the spiny surface below stands above the ground the same height as my horns, resulting in perfect painless support. Surprised I have no injuries but noticing I am stuck, one of the bearded dancers lifts me up and tosses me to the ground.

He looks at me suspiciously, causing my mask to come off, and I grab another from the same box he pushes over to me. The man that was behind me in line is now on the first horizontal log on the path to the flowing branch gate above. He flings both arms ahead at the same time to the next log, rather than swinging one arm and alternating, and falls down with tremendous force into the field of sharp things and howls in extreme pain. A dancing man from the other side looks at him in disdain yet lifts him from his misery and quickly heals him. The healed man walks past me into a cage that sits open nearby. The cage slides to the children who laugh and ridicule him. I am unable to see his reaction, but of course he is not at ease, so I call the children over to cross the logs. They run this way and up the steps, maskless, and impulsively jump towards the first log, all slipping down before grabbing any of the logs. None appearing terrified during the fall, they bounce from the sharp protrusions onto the ground, landing unharmed. Each puts on a mask and returns to the line on the steps.

I have a new mask with a detailed design of dots and dashes and a strong jaw that I feel deeper than the mask. Though less extravagant than the last, it is perfectly tight fitting and sleek…I am quick and agile. I join the children in line. The children look back to me and momentarily lift their masks above their faces to expose grave illnesses, each of them dangerously infected. They slide their masks back down, and anxious to get us all across, I prompt them to help me collect the short logs on the ground at the sides of the steps. They cooperate and we each place a new log across the two long outstretched logs, replacing the one the squirrel grabbed, and adding many more. Half of the children climb across the top and the other half of us swing from log to log on the bottom. We make it across to the opening of the highly anticipated heavenly branches. The children cannot go through it, but instead jump down to join the dancers, performing their own choreography…swaying side to side, energetically clapping. I step into the opening of the branches, but feel suffocated and cannot proceed. I am slowly lowered to the ground in the branches' embrace, and am again at the feet of the dancing men, with the children at their side.

Dancing in their perfect rhythmic stomps, they dress me in their masks, placing them all over me as I feel an array of life forces overcome me. As the children's faces are exposed, they reveal the disappearance of the diseases, now displaying healthy smiles and bright eyes on their rejuvenated faces. The children each take one of the masks I am wearing and rip the bottom off, placing the part covering the eyes and hair onto themselves, leaving the remainder on my body. Covered in many layers of masks, I sprint up the steps with the combined momentum of hundreds of wild creatures…flying over the platform to the logs, swinging across them effortlessly with unprecedented speed and agility. As I greet the dancers again, the children take over the dancing, keeping their own moves. The original dancing men with long hair and beards surround me and hold completely still. One of them rips the part of the mask that covers the bottom half of my face and tells me to eat well, before they together push me up into the portal of branches.

I walk through, breathing and moving well for many strides…I tumble forward and walk upside down for a while, and take several more walking strides…I see a barrier of familiar long wooden chutes ahead that suffocate me as I draw near. I avoid them, gaining my breath back, and walk a few miles more…mostly on my hands. I stop when I see a monstrous pile of much smaller versions of the same chutes, these the size of my finger. This obstruction forbids me to move through it and my ankles lock up as I buckle to the ground. I roll a handful of the thousands of tiny chutes over my body and the masks transfer from me onto the wooden tubes, wrapping tightly around them as they spring to life. The masks that cover the chutes in my hands, now living beasts, bounce to their feet pulling me with them, and those left behind fall underground. I turn and see the large wooden chutes, visible for many miles, recede into the ground and disappear behind me. Where this occurs, the dancing children rise from the soil and run towards me.

They come close and I see their actual organic faces are identical to the masks they wore. The man from the cage climbs from underground and approaches them, maddened with revenge in mind, and spits diseases at them. The power obtained by the children from the masks activates and visibly reflects the projected diseases back onto the man who falls backwards with his cage door slamming shut around him. He is sucked back into the ground and I hear heavy crashing, likely the huge wooden chutes piling onto his cage, assuring he will remain there forever.

Wearing the single remaining mask I saved from the awakenings of the tiny chutes, I have narrow eyes able to see a great distance, a strong bite, small wings, and a horn on my back…I am covered in many colors and jagged line patterns are drawn on me everywhere. The children and I touch one another's faces, fascinated by the infusions received from the masks. Like wild animals, we take off running as we endlessly leap on wooden log after wooden log, structured identically to the ones we previously encountered. The idea of slipping or falling never crosses our minds and we are filled with endless otherworldly joy. No diseases or shortness of breath invade us…we are healthy and strong. We grow tired from our run and fall into a canopy of the cozy branches awaiting below to catch us…we drift into a deep sleep and sleep a long peaceful night.

19. Mushroom Trench

I am walking with my legs spread over an empty trench with a container of sweet smelling liquid I am dumping into the space. The container is far superior to my own size, filled full, but I do not struggle to carry it and it does not feel heavy. The impact of liquid into the trench emits dense steam that rises, filling the air around me. This too smells sweet, best compared to lavender and apples with a touch of honey…the honey also descriptive of the consistency of the liquid I am pouring.

As I walk and continue to pour, the steam occasionally exposes parts of the ground, flashing a quick glimpse, like a cloak flying up in the wind and dropping down again. Delighted to at last be noticed, I see tiny fish eggs roll over and I witness a very long time ago passed on bird hold the last few minutes of his recognizable form, as he disintegrates into his equally old nest. I hop across large rocks and tree stumps that line the trench, with one foot on each side and my legs wide spread. The steam hovers over the rocks and stumps, eventually becoming them, and trusting I will land on something solid, I jump into the covering of steam. The steam feeds the rocks, stumps, the ground…all of it, quenching the thirst of all forms.

My eyes feel hydrated and my sight is vibrant and clear. Things begin falling into the trench I am still filling, first, a little white mushroom that I set down my container to pick up. It looks ordinary so I toss the mushroom aside and it lands upright, its stem impacting the ground with a loud POW accompanied by the sound of a large collapsing structure, of which I see no indication. The mushroom grows quickly as it forms dark spots, and remaining upright, it returns to the place in the trench from where it had been thrown. It expands into something that could shelter many creatures and part of its stem collapses, forming two doorways which the trench passes through. My container is back in hand, still full to the top with a river of its dispensed liquid flowing behind. I step through the doorway, and without stopping, I pour into the trench.

A new aroma of steam rises here and the liquid I pour spits up like hot oil into the tiny curves beneath the head of the mushroom. The oil spitting continues as I cease to pour and proceed out the other doorway. I see a flat piece of rubber covering the trench surface where I am next to pour. I reach to pick it up and the mushroom structure from behind rises up over my head and lands again before me, its doors invitingly open. Before I lift the rubber into the air, a vacuum force sucks it into the mushroom's interior, placing it on the ground. I fill the liquid where the rubber had been and I continue to the mushroom door. I step inside onto the rubber piece which drops down and kinks, folding and creasing itself into stairs…still only one footstep in, I am on the middle stair. I walk on through the mushroom, pouring no more inside. The dispensed liquid inside continues to pop like hot oil, splashing up through the rubber, outlining the intricacies under the mushroom cap, which has gotten noticeably larger.

I exit and walk again along the trench. I hear a heavy splash and look behind to see the mushroom submerge under the liquid, sliding beneath me underground and rising again in front of me. This time there are even more welcoming doorways, lavished with flowers and feathers and long strands of hanging herbs. The herbs fall into my container as I brush through them, and they soak up the rest of the liquid it contains. As they saturate, they sing "ooooooOOOoooooooo," like a choir of angels, making the flowers and herbs more fragrant, and the feathers fly like they are part of the same wings, yet by one another they remain untouched. The empty container falls into a whirlpool, dispensing it into the mushroom's center. The rubber piece follows, corking the hole and plugging it. The trench is now flowing with liquid, behind me and before me, as far as I can see. I look through the back door which I am soon to exit, and notice random items drifting in the liquid. Amongst many things, I pick up several loose keyboard keys, both black and white, and also some of other colors. I grab as many as I can hold and before I start walking, the mushroom falls over my head and I find myself again inside. A hammer falls, pounding the black and white keys onto the stairs that the rubber created. The whirlpool in the center, where the rubber washed away, is now disguised as a cooking pot containing a gruel-like substance, which seems to have erupted with the song. The few colorful keys join the herbs, flowers, and feathers around the doorway and the beautiful oo₀₀Oₒₒing angelic voice is now one with the sound of the keys, the music perfectly matching the singing.

I exit the back door of the mushroom and now even more items drift in the current of the liquid. The stumps are growing into trees…they trim themselves by bending over and knocking into the tallest rocks, the debris turning into the items floating around me. I see a tangled strand of tiny wheels release from a bush nearby and I pick it up. They collect into an organized group as they dive from my hands and gather at the base of the mushroom and quickly speed away. The song of the angels and the keyboard remain the same volume as the mushroom rolls far away. It disappears into the familiar heavy steam in the distance, and I instinctively reach for a long whip amongst the floating things and snap it far forward to the mushroom, cracking the whip around the wheels, pulling them away from beneath. I swim to the mushroom, which has come to an abrupt stop, and the honey-like fluid is like none I've ever touched. A basket of pure water with floating candles flows to me. I sip the water and sprinkle it into the air around me. The candles jump out and a modest fire rises on the trench's edges. I clear the trench, throwing the random strings, papers, empty boxes and such into the fire which it gladly accepts, sharing a polite roar of approval.

I continue swimming towards the mushroom, still hearing the soft "ooooooO" of the angels and the delicate sound of the keys. I find a kaleidoscope and through it, I view what is before me, and the scene itself dismantles as in the kaleidoscope view. The trench buckles and forms many small pools where the river of liquid had just been, enabling me to jump over them, as I approach my destination more quickly. Just before I reach the mushroom, the river resumes and the filled trench returns, knocking me into the black and white keys that cover the steps. I, too, make sounds that match the music, but I am not controlling it…my slippery feet are, though their offbeat slipping around motion does not at all match the smoothness of the sound they are creating.

The mushroom is growing in size and from the steps I am on, I can no longer see the backdoor as I could so easily from inside before. Along with the expansion it has developed a wobble, making its continued ability to reside on the trench unlikely. A steel balance clanks around the edge of the front step, so I reach to pick it up. The underside of the head of the mushroom sucks it up and from there retains its perfect balance and maintains its placement. A long line of blue marbles floats towards me, traveling in a perfectly spaced straight row as if attached to one another. I scoop them up and they spill on the floor inside the mushroom, lapping several times around the whirlpool in the center where I am certain they will drop. They radiate outward and flatten along the inside walls, forming impressive marble patterns, adding much beauty to complement the equally beautiful music.

I jump with excitement, feeling this contribute to the sounds around. Hot fire coals line the ceiling where the oil spitting occurred, and along with it comes a soft, nurturing warmth. The whirlpool in the center empties, splashing into the air…this provides a waterfall for the surface of the marble, now sculpted into finer form by the flying feathers. Steam projects from the center, soaking into everything around, giving it life. The feathers turn to mystical birds and the marble turns to gargoyles, spitting clean water into the center as it becomes steam. The angels rise from between the keys, fixing them into a full piano as they fly away. The air cools and I step above the center to breathe the warm steam. The steam unexpectedly pours onto me, pushing me down a hole. The original few stairs become many and I fall down them, but thanks to the angels, a few keys are left, covered in the honey-like liquid, protecting me from harm.

The mushroom slowly flies up like a large balloon. The piano created by the angels drops from it, landing directly under me, and I jump on the keys. I find a black blanket in the trench that I use to wipe the keys of the dirt, revealing their beautiful colors. I drape the blanket over it and it coats each key, wrapping tightly around it, making it all black. I climb up to see if the sounds are the same. They are, but the tones resonate longer, I discover, as I find myself high in the sky, inside the mushroom, still rising. A backpack slips over my arms onto my shoulders and I am again dispensed through the center of the mushroom. As I fall to the ground, I shuffle ideas of how to fill the hole and I truly hope the piano will push me to the mushroom's increasing height. I am thinking of the rubber that worked so well to cork the hole, and about this backpack that just saved me from impact. I open the bag to find an apple-lavender-honey smelling liquid. I empty it into the trench and a small cupped dome of rubber turns inside out, flips high up, and cups the bottom of the hole with its tight suction. I climb onto the piano to return to the mushroom, finding it does indeed still launch me high enough. I discover the mushroom has reached new ground far above, just high enough for the piano to propel me. I sit in the center on top of the bowl of rubber that cups the hole from beneath. Steam releases, falling abundantly below, and I jump off with the downpour. The ground and the trench are well moistened. I sit to catch my breath and lay my head on the backpack full of liquid as I prepare to stand up and keep pouring.

20. Giant Potion

There is very foamy water in front of me. A woman from behind steps ahead, walking right through me, and slaps it down with the bottom of her hands, presumably to eliminate the bubbles. I tell her she is doing it wrong and that she is going to cause more bubbles to form. She ignores me and surely enough, the water becomes overwhelmed with tiny foamy bubbles. With the intention of counteracting her doings, I wisp the bubbles up with my forearms into the air. The number of bubbles drastically increases as they rise, turning into detailed live scenes throughout the sky. The first is a glorious castle with an extreme moat containing the deadliest sharks swimming the deep waters, hungry to swallow anything alive. Second, a violin quartet with an audience of listeners captivated by their song, each grasping a book and holding their finger in place of their page to watch the performers. Other pictures paint the sky, and my attention is drawn to the negative space, becoming imagery in itself as it steps forth into a new dimension…it collapses down, turning into branches, breaking through the painted scenes in the sky.

The branches don't seem like they can get any closer, but they do, they do, they do, and I keep expecting to touch them, but I don't…they keep rushing down as closer becomes redefined each time. Now a vision so huge that I can only see two branches that have turned magnificently large since being of the thousands of tiny ones I could see racing towards me moments ago. Still unable to touch one, I lift off my toes and jump in an attempt. I succeed, hugging the trunk with my arms stretched around it as far as they can go, wrapped around just enough to hang on, leaving most of its circumference untouched. I hang on the gigantic branch, falling towards the Earth, each moment more baffled by the fact that I haven't yet crashed into the ground. I climb up thrusting at my core, legs and arms clung to the tree, alternating force between them as I climb as fast as I can. I maneuver through more branches and now I have surely climbed many miles when my head dips into a body of water above me.   I fall directly backwards, back and legs straight.

I am standing with my feet wet in the body of water that I just encountered above with my head. I see a gigantic tree, even greater in magnitude than it appeared before, but surely it is the same one…although this time it is growing up, not falling. It begins to collapse and I hear, "Timmmberrrrr!" and I am suddenly in the dark with a soft oddly shaped shelter around me, heated and very warm inside. Growing uncomfortably hot, I gasp for air that returns as an echo instructing something mysterious that I don't understand, but am sure to remember. The structure removes itself and I am in the light again. The tree is gone and I see what had just surrounded me, climbing onto it to examine it further. It again moves, jostling me up and down as it plops on the ground, each time occupying a distance farther ahead than the last, as I remain on the structure.

I am elevated into the air as something of the same material grabs me with a hard pinch on the back of my neck. I splash into a giant container of bubbly fluid with a large pole that floats freely, shifting angles. I examine my surroundings, thankful I can swim and am currently endowed with unlimited underwater breath. A giant face appears from above, wraps his lips around the pole, and sucks up the water around me. He drops his wide eye into the opening above, as if to examine me. He says, "I thought that was you," and tells me that he will do as instructed and apologizes that I am unable to stay and that he is powerless in that determination despite his efforts in anticipation of my arrival. He drops me into a larger container, even large considering his giant of all giants' stature. I see a girl there and the water is very foamy. We play, popping the bubbles, and have a lot of fun. We talk of making a potion to bring trees to our container. I remember the secret recipe from the mumble from afar, heard while I was beneath the hot covering, surely to have come from the giant as I was under his foot.

21. Running with Paws

A black bat monster with a large wingspan drops from the sky in a quick fall with open arms, hungry for a capture…his conniving grin boasts anticipation of grabbing one of the many young ones walking together on this dark night. He flaps his wings into the ground, hovering over the children, and curls them up to his body, ready to fly away with as many as he can. Most of the children kick from his hold and escape, running away in every direction. Fortunately his large wings lack precision on swiping them up individually once they have scattered. The bat succeeds in capturing the youngest ones, unable to run as quickly. As he lifts, a carriage rolls into him and cripples his right wing, both releasing the little ones and inhibiting his ability to fly. He crawls into a small space between the ground and a cement area buried below with large holes stuffed with snouts of mysterious wolf-like creatures sniffing out from them. Below the transparent dirt on the ground, he slides between the snouts easily, hunching with his limp injured wing.

As he looks back to me over his frail shoulder, I see into his mouth…discovering he has a baby in its hold. I run with all my speed to catch the injured bat, escaping underground where I can easily see him. Snout after snout nips up at the bat, sniffing into the air, as the wolves become more aggressive to bite their way out of the cement area they are trapped in.   My running shakes the ground and the wolf creatures bark like blood thirsty dogs. Finally one breaks out, now in the same layer as the bat, between his recent prison and the ground beneath. With his ears smashed down, he sniffs and stays under me as I keep running. His own hostility escalates as he further attempts to break from this surface.

Many wolves are breaking from their original layer as they fight to free themselves through the hole their fellow wolf had made. The vigorous competition for exit causes congestion and many injuries, therefore many forfeit and drop back down from where they came. The ones that do make it up chase the bat, still in sight, as they bark in unison with a shared goal, like a wolf pack catching dinner. The bat stops and turns around to those coming after him, showing them the baby in his mouth. The wolves do not stop and as they reach him, the bat turns to the right and flings his left wing towards them, slicing each of their necks. He continues running, still with the baby, this time much faster and I start to lose sight of him.

The wolves, seriously injured, all lay on their backs with their paws straight up. The bottom of them push opposite my feet that drop harder and harder, pushing to run faster. Holes form in the ground and I feel their paws on the soles of my feet as they speed me ahead. Their paws wrap around my toes and I feel a suction pulling us closer. Their legs swing back and forth in rhythm, all together, catching me perfectly as I land on them…working with my strides as if we are all one entity. They lie beneath me, row by row, their heads pointed the direction I am moving. Their back legs catch me and push me up past their heads, passing me up to the next, moving me quickly towards the bat I pursue.   I have not had him in sight for some time, so I work hard to move faster until I finally see something ahead, unable to identify what.

Red orchid-like flowers grow along the narrow space I am approaching and broken glass is scattered heavily throughout the passage. It must be from the wolves breaking out, who somehow got ahead of me. Now as they run towards me I realize that I have been running without their help for quite some time and their group is what I recently observed ahead…not the bat as I had hoped. I am happy to see the wolves, however, feeling grateful for their assistance. They continue towards me, entering the field of the red orchids that lies ahead. I step foot into the field and trip and fall, landing in a pile of the wolves rolling around on the ground. I pleasingly roll with them, smearing red all over us. We do this until we are tired and as I try to leave, a wolf bites my leg so that I cannot go. It is not severe and causes no pain but it is bleeding profusely. The wolf coaxes me back to the pile of his pack and along with them, I drift off to sleep.

I wake easily to soft footsteps coming towards us that I identify as those of the bat, holding the baby tucked under his injured wing. I do not reveal that I am awake, and in my false slumber he comes to lick my wolf bite and his wing rises, apparently healed. The baby drops and the bat goes to tuck it away in a burrow nearby. He sneaks up to the wolves, smeared red with orchid, and prepares to devour them. I leap forward to grab the baby in the burrow, and start running…the bat immediately notices and takes off after me.

The wolves wake and sprint towards us in the underground space below. They catch up to me and again push their paws up from below, working to move me at least quadruple my normal speed, launching me far ahead with each push from their strong legs below. I look down as I flee with the baby, further and further away from the bat, and see pieces of the bat being chewed by the wolves below me. I assume they got him, but I keep running to be sure.

Babies and very young children begin falling from the sky, most with minor cuts or injuries. Some fall from the arms of their parents that have just passed on, whose spirits rise into the clouds as they leave their bodies behind. Between the ground and the clouds, an invisible surface catches these bodies as their souls rise out of sight. Just as the babies are about land, this platform of unoccupied bodies releases several loose arms that fall down and attach onto me, enabling me to catch every baby. They grow quickly, all able to run holding one of my many hands, which increase in number as time goes on, along with the falling babies from the sky.

The same bat returns to his flight overhead, this time mainly wings, most of his body having been chewed away by the wolves. He swings down and captures a child running behind, the only one without one of my arms to hold. His weak mouth that now barely exists, soon drops the boy from its bite. A wolf springs from the ground to catch the child on his back and runs with him, easily catching up to me. The wolf howls and I see a spirit, mostly man resembling wolf, in the layer where the bodies are left on their way to the heavens. He cuts his arm off and tosses it down to me where it attaches, extending from my forehead. On its own, without my command, this arm reaches behind me and grabs the boy from the wolf's back. The wolf jumps high into the air, howling at the pale moon in the day sky…and captures the bat between his sharp teeth. I stop and cover the children with my blanket of arms.

The wolf meanwhile mimics the movement of the bat just before he eats it. He comes to me as I protect the children, and lays his head on top of mine. He gradually climbs all of the way on top of me, slowly, as if acting on his dreams as we all rest. I fall asleep and wake to many baby wolf cubs feeding on my wolf breasts…The wolf brings us a very large black animal to eat, an animal I have never seen, but it tastes better than anything I've ever had. I keep our babies covered, safely protected under me, as I see bats fly around the pale moon in the sky…many wolves around us start to howl.

22. Wicker People

Euphoria continues as I dance in circles jumping high as I ever have, basking in the perfect heat of the sun. The buildings, along with the few other things scattered about, like lamp posts and wicker baskets, enlarge as I exhale and shrink as I inhale, sometimes moving with a strong enough breath. I inhale hard enough to pull a wicker basket towards me. It opens and I jump in. The lamp posts all turn on and I ascend in the wicker basket by the heat of the lamps. The basket starts to fall and I blow far down to heat the lamps beneath me. It seems to work and I ascend again in the basket. Everything is bright and I can hardly see as I near the sun. Flocks of crows come down, moving their wings frantically to shield me with their dark color from the sun. I sneeze and they are scared away…but that's ok, they were very nice to me, but I like the bright sun better.

I am distracted by the crows and I again fall in the wicker basket. I am alone on the ground away from the basket and I wonder where it is. I look up attempting to find it and I stop to admire the sun. I look at it for a few moments, blinking my eyes…a few seconds opened and a few seconds closed, until I can no longer tell the difference. The sun now has a black hole in its center. Since open and closed eyes feel the same to me, I rapidly blink to ensure I am receiving the sun's image from both sides. The black hole is now gone…it must have been the wicker basket's shadow and there is really no black hole at all. I continue jumping, skipping, spinning, all of the fun motions that comprise my dance.

I breathe, the growth and shrinking of the items are again synchronized. I inhale a large vine too strongly, intending to pull a wicker basket towards me, and I choke on it. I lay back, re-grasping my consciousness. As the choke sorts itself out, I withdraw my efforts and relax. This time I am certain there is a hole in the center of the sun. Wicker baskets from above pour people onto the sandy surface, and their feet sink so far down they can no longer run. They are cold, but dressed in many clothes, more than I.

Three men who have fallen in the sand are entangled in one another, their arms and legs tied together…they tell me to come over before the sun gets me too. Annoyed by their threat, I walk over anyway. Seeing they are cold and miserable, I cover their unified being with a blanket I have draped over my back. Suddenly I am cold, but much colder than the loss of the blanket ought to have caused me. The three men tell me, each rotating their words to together create sentences, that they were on their way to pick up the material. "What material?" I ask, "I have given you a blanket, what else do you need?" They reluctantly tell me, each disclosing a word at a time to reveal the entire situation, that they were on an expedition to the sun to acquire a rare wicker material, invisible to the naked eye, in order to connect the Earth just a little closer to the sun. The purpose of this, the second darkest man goes on to say, is to increase the daily temperature in order to continue the Earth's ability to support human life. You see, I measure the men in darkness because there is one dark black, one stark white, and one just in the middle.

Having spent so much time near the sun, they have adapted to high heat…now back on Earth they are cold but encumbered with flames and they begin to die. An instant before his death, the medium colored man hands a coin to the very white man who continues on to say, "Wicker, 48, 5,150…material, distance, and strength." I go on to repeat to ensure my understanding and he too, dies before he can acknowledge my understanding. The dark man says, "48, not any closer," as he dissolves into flames, taking his mates with him.

I return to my skipping until I breathe as hard as I can, with a goal to summon all wicker baskets. They slowly but surely draw nearer to me and I disassemble them, completing this with the fluid motion of dancing with my arms. I unweave 48 of them, panting heavily to draw each one to me, and taking over the men's task, I connect the material into a long cord, in an effort to tie the Earth closer to the sun. To form the knot, I wrap the cord around the remnants of the three men, twisting it tightly around their ribs, one of the few parts of them that remains. Certainly the ribs are a permanent part of the Earth now, I think, as deep lava gathers around their ashy limbs and solidifies, binding them to the Earth's surface. I climb the wicker material collected from the 48 baskets, and face the sun to make the final connection.

The lava carries the spirit of the men up to me, as it covers the rope of wicker, strengthening it. I work my hands to eliminate the wicker's kinks and guide it through the sun's central hole and back out again, weaving it through the sun 5,150 times. I slide down the shaft that has been created, breathing heavily…this time more naturally from working so hard, and a multitude of wicker baskets approaches me. Masses of people exit the baskets, defying the physical ability of so many fitting into them, and they celebrate the warmth of the sun for days.

After a few days, one basket arrives delivering a warm blanket, heated by the rays of the sun. I continue to skip and dance and love my sweat, remembering how cold I'd always been before. Now, from the grasp of my hands, the blanket rises in flames…but I am far from too hot.

23. Air Flags

I am in a vertical cylindrical tube approximately four times my length but just barely wide enough for me to fit. There is nothing holding me in place but I bounce around slightly to rebalance my body in the center, buoyant, as in water, when the speed of the vessel shifts. I can see out in every direction…the round circular wall surrounding me is completely clear like there is nothing between me and the air, although the tightness of it restrains my arms, prohibiting most motion.

The two flat planes of glass, several feet above and below me, are colored with a myriad of intense but uninterpretable symbols, composed of every color…they, too, are translucent, allowing me to see through them. Above me the designs in the glass shift subtly, in conjunction with the movement of the clouds, also of varied colors in mysterious shapes. The round glass tightly hugging me makes my head's range of motion minimal, so I roll my eyelids far down to get a better look at the bottom. At the full stretch of my extreme glance, I see a surface beyond the glass below me that I will soon land on. Upon releasing the strain of my eyes, they remain locked in a fully extended downward position. The intricate pattern of the transparent colors starts to bubble, my eyes inevitably fixed on only this. The lines of the design move around, complicit with the bubbling, shifting in a certain pattern, working as if to open a lock…until the bottom glass panel breaks open and disappears, dropping me onto hot desert sand.

I rub my eyes as they pour out streams of sand, now released from their immobility. Relieved, I direct my attention upward to a circle of more flagpoles than I could possibly count, waving above me, surrounding me in its large center. I run the inside circumference before remembering the intention of doing so, and it takes me one hundred twenty two seconds, as I count in my head. The perimeter of the circle holds so many flags that it is impossible to lay eyes on each one, even only briefly. Each bears a unique detailed pattern of unfathomable eccentricity.

I recognize the patterns in the flags as identical to those on the top ceiling of the tube I arrived in. I recall the glass displaying alternating images which are now before me. On one flag, I see the image that trapped my eyes downward to its sight, and suddenly I am put in a trance and I cannot shift my focus. The image bubbles discreetly, reminiscing the attitude of the sizzling floor that dropped me here. At the first opportunity I feel strong enough to break from the trance, I quickly turn my eyes and "SNAP!" I hear the flagpole drop like a big branch falling from a high tree. I instantly react, rushing towards it in time to catch its tip before it hits the ground. The bubbles crawl from the flag onto my hand and burn me. I drop it, my eyes follow it down, and I am again locked in a downward glance. I hear the whips of the other flags crack strongly in the air, delivering a cool breeze that relieves my hands.

I reach to rub my eyes again but find I am holding two statues, both of old women, one in each hand. The statue in my right hand shakes in my palm and tiny groups of constructed hand and forearm bones emerge from her head and without hesitation, they dive into my eye socket and reorient my eyesight. The bones retract into the woman and her head grows until it breaks away into the air as tiny specks of dust. These emit a high frequency sound like tiny obnoxious insects, but the noise disappears as they collect onto the bubbling flag, still at my feet. The statue in my left hand jumps into the pile of black dust, also emitting the high frequency sound, and the pole stands again. The flag is restored with no bubbles, again displaying one of the many breathtakingly complex designs.

I walk to the flagpole beside the one that fell and rose and the same black dust falls from it into my eyes. I freeze and watch it sprinkle down from the flag above me until my sight is completely relinquished and the shrill sound volumes increase. The flags again snap through the wind, creating pockets of air that release different types of waves and sounds as they overcome my senses. I feel like my eyes are closed but I can see the pockets of air, coded in colors grouped by speed, particle density, and force of movement. I am unable to

see the flags, their poles, or the desert sand of the
environment I am in, but the collection of sounds is the
clearest, strongest stimulus I have ever felt. The flags
smack air vivaciously, perpetuating the flow of different
air types that move independently from one another.
They further develop their unique form of motion and
intensity of color as each moment passes.

The flags' movement gradually softens and the
pieces of dust freely flying through the air sort
themselves, moving to their respective blocks of air.
Their forms change to unify with the gases around them.
Some fluff up like clouds and join the purple air, with its
energy waves gracefully churning back and forth,
occupying the same general area of space with what is
similar. Some go to the red air which spits and crackles,
jerking around chaotically infiltrating the spaces of the
others. Gold dust occupies the section of air that I am
breathing, moving both up and down in its modest area
of space, like two hourglasses pouring quickly in
opposite directions. I watch new colors and patterns
form, filling new sections as they develop. The black

dust particles adapt their sound, movement, and form to whatever group they join, evenly distributing throughout the spaces. As the energies of dust join their section, they develop a certain sound…all of which are pleasant except for the red at its highest energy point and the little spaces between the air pockets where the unassigned black dust turns stale, releasing painful shrieking sounds that generate disturbing echoes.

I reach for the black dust near me, it disappears, and the flag waves stop. Everything turns silent and still, the colors and motion maintaining great intensity beyond the stillness. The black dust falls from the areas where it is trapped, back into my eyes, and I can see again. Deeply connected with the life energy of this atmosphere, I now see the colors on the flags match the attitude of the lines they create. Now I also understand that the air of different colors flows through tiny holes on each flag, creating its pattern.

Smiling and feeling a refreshing pleasure from the gold dust I breathe, I walk outside the circle and see the pockets of air in their familiar motions, creating the essence of the flags. A flagpole again falls down, this time one completely blank without color, movement, design or anything. I jump into the circle in time to catch it, guiding it to land with its top to the outside of the border, and it becomes an intricately designed flag. Black dust covers it and the image disappears. I yell, "NOOOO!" reacting to the loss of its perfect energy, and the colored winds activate, stirring around and steeping into the holes on the blank flag. Seeing this effect, I use a range of vocal tones, calling the different colored gases to the flag as they stain it with their color, drawing lines by speed and curves from density…designing the flag.

The other flags wave again, pulling the new one towards them. The new flag turns red and sparks, so I pull it backwards, releasing it from the pole as I tumble back, wrapped in it. I feel it bubbling and warming me like I am being nurtured and massaged by an indulgent hot liquid. My eyes roll upward in bliss and I see a clear ceiling above, exchanging similar flag-like images on its surface. I continue "painting" the one around me, sounding different tones. I look around to find I'm wrapped in a mass of these powerful flags, generating their energy with the moving groups of wind that design the flags above, below, and all around me. I see the groups of air around me by their sound, visually identifiable by color and motion. I feel myself dissipate into the energy…breaking off into pieces, disassembling into the energy fields…until from them I can no longer distinguish myself.

24. Ladder Layers

The shelf moves away from me as I place the last item upon it. As it moves I continue reaching for it, my toe tips sticking to the wall behind me, stretched out as far as my whole body can reach. I slowly fold in backwards to my toes as my muscles release the tension they have acquired.

A bit earlier, I assembled items along with a group of people, designing them point by point as we passed them along. No purpose of the items had been discussed as we constructed the designs. As each item was finished, it was placed on a shelf that dunked backwards into a glossy pool that churned, rotating the items slowly in the goo until they changed form completely. Then a lever was pulled and each item buried.

Now I sit reviewing what I have done and I feel the memories slip quickly. The highest part of my head shakes so I lay my forehead down. Below me is a rainbow colored ladder, each step rotating in one of 'many possible directions. I step onto the first rung and its motion automatically sends me down to the next. The next one flips me around over and over, all the way around with the bottom of my arches clinging to the step. The rungs above and below me easily stretch to accommodate this rotation. After doing this for a long time, my legs wear down and snap off like twigs. I fall down the ladder, skipping a few steps, catching myself a few rungs down with my hands.

I am on a bright yellow step, brighter than any yellow I have seen before, and I see many small winged creatures I hadn't noticed on my ladder climb thus far. They cover me with tiny wet leaves that with their soft push, stick to my skin. My skin tingles, but I can't feel exactly where, like the sensation is on a part of me that does not physically exist. The little flying fairies intermix into small groups, each tending to a certain part of my body with the leaves. As the leafy layer builds, they weave in and out of them, tying them together with one another's hair. When they go behind the leaves, it feels like they have crossed into my skin, and the tingling stops. Some are trapped behind the leaves as others unintentionally tie them in with strands of hair. I feel them wiggle around a while until I experience an intense energy release. They fall down either my spine or ribs, depending on their original position, and exit at the bottom of my waist where my legs have broken off. As this occurs, I feel a force counteract the hanging of my arms, like some invisible pressure is pushing me up, reducing the ongoing strain of my hang. Each one that ends up here looks up to me, smiles, and happily flies away…leaving two of them behind in her place. They slowly melt into me as our sensations collide and we become one another.

My legs are growing back, crowding the ladder rung below me, so I use my arms to climb to the next rung up, which I missed the first time down due to my fall. I have arrived to a new layer with dimmer light, and I hear wings fluttering about as before. With a hard look, I recognize some of the same fairies that had buried themselves into the leaves they gave me on the bright yellow rung, but this time they are all struggling, missing physical parts…eyes, entire faces, or a wing, all inhibiting their comfort to a great degree. I feel a cold sensation on my toes, shocked by the feeling of having legs and feet, like I never had them before. My memory reminds me of them, but now my legs are much longer and I have no sensory recollection of how to use them. I feel the tickle of the wings below my feet pushing me upward, and I am back on the ladder rung with my old broken off legs. My new legs stand upon my old ones, which are being aggressively eaten by birds, and they fall down with the birds still pecking at them. I reach down to grab them with my arms that can suddenly expand to limitless lengths, and I catch them as they almost fall to the ground. I see the bottom of the ladder for the first time.

Its base is propped up in a pool of dirty boiling water with birds falling into it, never able to fly out again. They live to feed on the body parts on the muddy surface, with a hop here and there as they jump on the boil. I return to the layer of the decrepit fairies, my old legs in hand. They pick at them with their tiny fingers, each claiming a fair section, working cooperatively. The skin, blood, bone, and ligaments become the body part that each one is missing. The light comes, the dim dry air disappears, and the flying people are now glowing, fully assembled and happy. Most of them bring me bouquets of leaves tied together with their hair. I inhale them to enjoy the scent, and they disappear as I feel jolting and expansion in my brain. I can suddenly see more and remember everything, and with far superior understanding than ever before. I look down, observing that I am still covered in leaves, and fall down the ladder in the path of my sight…the leaves keeping me protected from the dirty boiling water I finally fall into.

From the hot muddy pool, I break down the ladder, noticing its intricacies that I remember designing, and the water turns clear. The birds fly away, and dust falls from them that sticks to the body parts that sunk to the bottom of the pool at the turn of the clear water. I jump from the pool to walk away, looking behind as I move steps ahead, and see people arise from the pool that last contained only body parts. They run faster to me as I notice them, and each asks me to build a random item to help them start a new life. We cooperatively sit in a circle and get to work. We are surrounded by many shelves that contain unrecognizable things, but each thing is somehow exactly what we need...

25. Swan Sea

A North American Indian comes to me with a long face, appearing as if he'd been crying. He is covered in many clothes but comes close and says he is terribly cold and that he has spilled his rice and is now alone and hungry. His family disappeared, he tells me, and he is keeping them close by wearing all of their clothes he could find. He removes his robe, wrapping it around me, and rolls up his multiple sets of long sleeves to show me the bracelet that his oldest daughter made when she was young…and she had always kept it on since, he tells me. I notice many images drawn up his arm, including a basket filled with corn and many reptiles. I compliment the beauty of the art and he tells me that he wishes it were a basket of rice instead, and snakes…and that he wishes his family were praising the art, not me.

He gives me a large wooden spoon and guides me to the shore, silent until he mutters the word, "wait." Another spoon washes up to me, now I have one in each hand and I use them to paddle to a small island in sight, careful not to hit the swans, which cover the water entirely. The man is swimming behind me, using antlers as his oars. I arrive at the island and step onto the ground…the flat backs of large beasts, hunched over, dipping their faces into overflowing bowls of rice.

A woman smiles and waves me over as she stirs a large pot while having her hair braided by a very young girl who is standing on a chair because she is afraid of the beasts on which we are standing. The legs of the chair break the beast's skin, and the liquid excess from his insides, a brownish black, leaks into the ocean and he grunts with discomfort. The woman's hair is fully braided down to her ankles and she turns around and puts the little girl down, who becomes a baby beast herself. The woman picks up the chair to relieve the creature in pain, and is suddenly embracing the Indian man. He undoes her braid and it becomes a robe he puts on. My spoons fall into the boiling pot of water that the woman had been stirring, and sensing the man's terror, I jump in after them. Here, a zipper on my back unzips and I slide out of my skin, gaining the ability to swim quickly to the bottom.

On the rocky bottom, many children are sitting in straw hats holding hands in a circle, some whispering to one another in the ear. One young boy breaks from the circle and tells me, whispering in my ear, that the women in the circle center stole from him and now he has nothing. The other children hold completely still until he returns to his place, which he refuses to do until I step into the center. I do this with no hesitation. Once I am in the circle, I take a leaf that is given to me by the eldest child and put it under my tongue, and immediately another woman comes and asks me for it. I refuse and she pours hot soup on me. The second woman of the two, tells me to name all of the children and that she weeps every day at her inability to address them. Realizing I am losing my breath, I do not respond.

I look to the children around me, all blowing up balloons. The young child who approached me before hands me a filled balloon which I try to untie, but I can't. I remove the leaf from under my tongue and then it unties easily, and I breathe in the air which it contains. The first woman who before wanted my leaf comes back and picks up the leaf I have now expelled onto the ground. She smiles and gives me two wooden spoons. The children stand up, disassemble their circle, and form a line in front of me, each placing their balloon on me after untying it and giving me the air inside. My skin returns piece by piece with each balloon. I am reconstructed but desperately thirsty so the second woman brings me a pitcher of water. I drink it quickly and wake on the back of a huge swan.

I wash ashore, shivering, greeted by a family who clothes my scarred skin with a robe. In thanks, I give them two spoons which bring tears to their eyes, and they make rice in a bowl of their collected tears. They all have a bowl except for me. Feeling mysteriously overjoyed, I remove a gold bracelet from my wrist, approach the youngest girl and clasp it to her wrist, as I smile and say, "Here, this is yours now." I walk away and tuck myself under the wing of the biggest swan, and place my face just under the water. The brownish black substance from the pierced beast coats my skin, making it water proof, and now the water is clean and I can finally breathe.

26. Cut in the Face of Fire

I am shaking my head from side to side, pushing the slight pain I have away from my center of focus, because I feel I have a way to go before I am safe. Though I appear to be outside, I see distant angled walls that meet at a pointed ceiling far above. Long blades are slicing down from it, cutting away at the black leathery ground I am on…most of the time landing away from me except for the most recent strike that I am recovering from, a diagonal slash across my body. My blood drips as I run to the edge of the black leathery surface, and I find colored rings of the same texture concentrically surrounding me…first a tan color then green then blue…beyond that it looks black again into the distance.

The dropping blades mostly fall outside of the blue ring into the outer black space, occasionally landing within, having previously struck me once. The pain from this has now subsided but blood is still dripping. I feel relatively safe despite the close blows of some of the blades cutting sharply above me, but thankfully they now always land in the far away black. My blood soaks into the leather ground on contact, fully disappearing as soon as it drops. As I run through the tan area, the color border shifts and what once was a smooth circle leading into the green, turns into serrated star-like outlines. I stand at this sector and look ahead to a river of white, surrounding the blue ring to separate it from the black in the distance. I see clear hoses running red with my blood, feeding out from the colored rings through the white river, connecting to the wide open black space beyond. A horde of fleas and ticks marches from the outskirts of the black towards the white water, expecting to sip the blood, I imagine.

I hear a subtle drum beat in the distance that turns into a conglomeration of drummers, coming nearer as indicated by the increasing sound, however I do not see any sign of them…just the oversized morbid black ticks and fleas, thirsty for blood. I step to the edge of the blue and the ground shifts, nearly pushing me into the white river. The colored section, with its small black center, rises up to create a dome. I am on the down slope of the dome and the invaders are close to both the blood tubes and now me. I reach down in an effort to lift the hoses, but I slip down, now straddling one of them, close enough to a tick to look him in the eye. The blades quicken with the pace of the drum and the hoses break from the black and rise with the crest of the developing dome. The wide open black land, now infested with fleas and ticks, drops further with each cut of the blades before lifting up over the white water and the colored rings…off like a shirt thrown from a body…up over my head and tossed away.

It falls atop four tall posts, arranged in a corner around a freshly lit fire. I smell something of an acidic nature and see the fleas and ticks harden into a plastic-like covering, melting away in a quick sizzle of burning steam. This better exposes the black surface they were on and I now unmistakably observe it as an animal's hide. The disappearance of the black pests and the power of the fire radiate the hide into a copious bundle of fur. I am still on the colored rings, able to stay on the dome with the help of the blood hoses. The sound of the drummers is accompanied now by their faces, all enormous compared to my miniature size. They arrive one by one and sit around the fire, admiring the hide on the posts high above them. The drumming quickens and a beautiful olive skinned woman with dark features takes the hide off the posts around the fire and places it on her back. The hair from it crawls up her back, settling into her own hair, and her head moves every direction in a rapturous sway.

The fire has now risen to a distance far above where the hide sat. The woman kicks her feet straight out and in this stance jumps onto the pillars, now centered within the fire, and lands on her back. About half of the drummers continue while the others stop to chant and sing in a language I cannot translate, but the emotion of it explains enough. Whispers and divinely powered winds wisp around the fire as the woman maintains a peaceful yet wild expression and burns away in an embrace of magical chants and spirits. Her body's outer surface crumbles as ash into the fire below, and an inner layer is exposed and rebirthed…remaining protected by the fur that dances in the spirit's song around her.

From the small black circle in the very center of my domed platform that I now sit upon, I see a man come near me as he maintains his drum beat. On the way he stops to put one of his drum sticks in the hand of the burning woman, keeping his beat with the other. Not noticing my miniature form, he yanks a blanket from under me and I fall onto a tall copper candlestick, remaining on the dome surface…my feet on the black, surrounded by the tan, then the green and the blue, all colors still intact. Now what was above is outward towards the fire, and the candlestick holds me and the dome I am on from below.

A few men step around the woman and place one of their drum sticks onto her, the first one into her other hand and the rest lined across her heart. They continue playing with one hand, and working together, they each use their free hand to lift a large wooden board and place it as a platform beneath the woman. They lift her away and set her beside the fire and along with the other drummers, both men and women and some children, they kneel around her. Together, they sing a new chant and the fire stretches up to the sky in the shape of a spiral. The sound of ocean waves emerges to accompany the chanting and drums. The man sitting at the crown of the woman folds the hide over to expose her face, now only a flat layer of skin with no features.

The two smallest children each tip over one of the two candlesticks, and still on the dome, I tumble down. The surface I am on, now more like a ball, and the other ball from the other candlestick, bounce onto the woman's face, tucking under the hide towards the top of her head. I hear whispers and singing from inside the fire, and those gathered join in, many still beating their drums. Everything shakes and I feel the woman's forehead raise up, bobbing up and down with the sound of her own drum beat she has just begun. Through the light of the fire beyond the hide that covers me, I see the kneeling people jump high in celebration.

A man with a blade slices the hide from the top of her face, leaving the top of her head and back untampered. He leaves the balls from the candlesticks undisturbed, the one I am on still dangling with blood-filled hoses, and they naturally roll into the incisions he has created. I have a small cut from the blade that cleared the woman's face and the free end of a hanging hose attaches to my wound to refill itself. I feel my energy pour from me and the hoses plant themselves into the new eye socket of the woman. She feeds the drum stick in her left hand to the fire and I fall down her face…past her newly formed soft nose and delicately curved mouth, knocking a drum stick from her heart into her left hand. Again holding two drumsticks, one freshly fallen from her heart, she plays a majestic tune that enchants all around the fire as they join her song.

After a dancelike fall down her gorgeous form, I land at her feet, noticing I am about the size of her toe. I climb into an incision in the woman's foot from which a red hose protrudes. I touch it and it clings to my finger, connecting us. I am suddenly climbing out from behind her eye as if I had been forever stuck on it, and she now sets me free…releasing me into the fire with the spirits still alive within it.

27. Sun Map

I am on a walk unsure of the time of day and where the darkness is going or whether it is still yet to come. I see the sun and moon in the sky at the same time, not beside each other or in different parts of the sky, but layered on top of one other, unclear of which is over the other. I continue to walk, in search of my intention…my purpose for this walk is presently unclear, though I can sense its importance. The ground is uneven and rocky, covered with things waiting to be tripped on or agitated, but the concentration I have on the sun and moon forbid me any accidents. The wind blows and for the first time, my sight is broken from the wonder in the sky…I catch a piece of paper that displays a map, along with my moving mirror image.

I pull the map close to my face to focus on the geography, only lightly penciled on the paper, as I involuntarily look back at my own gaze that dominates the map. There is no trail, map key, or any indication of deciphering the meaning of the strange map, unrecognizable in every way. Staring into the focal point of my own reflective pupils, the eyes on the map move independently from mine. They jump off the mirror face and gaze peculiarly, moving to different points on the nearly empty map, merely an outline indicating water and forests in a few places. The territory is mapped as a messy circle, many parts falling outside of a typical 360 degree circle. The circle is broken at the top, the rest of it connected. My reflected eyes, still separated from its face, move downward together, the force of movement coming from the outside corner of each eye, scooting them along.

My source of vision, my own eyes, are still moving independent of those on the map, so I watch closely and pull charcoal from my pocket to trace the path of the eyes on the map. They move down a bit further, and sit still to the south-east of where the main forest is marked, south of their prior location. The stillness of the eyes breaks into intense movement as they shake, building up and harnessing some kind of powerful energy. The eyes tense as the eyelids move drastically upward, as if trying to communicate some sort of sincere message to me. Sensing the eyes as those of a stranger, I mimic the sincerity with my own eyes and draw nearer for a deeper look. As I come close, the eyes rapidly blink and turn to flesh…teeth break through the paper, piercing it with a threatening bite as it ferociously strikes towards me. A sinister man with long jagged widely spaced blood stained teeth pushes through the paper of the map. I reach into my pocket for my axe, and chop the top half of his head off at the middle of his nose bridge. He falls back into the paper, his eyes soften, and they revert to those seen as my own reflection.

The eyes on the map now rest near the series of holes the jagged teeth left as the man was breaking from the world behind the map. I put my hand to my face wondering what reflection the map will display of it, and seeing nothing, I find I have a small amount of hot blood on my cheek. The arrangement of blood dots directly corresponds with the holes on the map. I drag my fingers over the holes, smearing the dots of blood between them. Doing this, I have a quick moment to ponder their perfect match before I am sucked through the holes…feet, hands, and head first, folded in half at the waist. I am now on the other side with larger holes in the same pattern cut into my body…I feel cold air go through them, occupying most of my feeling. I find the man again on this side, this time serene. I am holding the map but now it feels sturdy, with no holes and no trace of blood. My reflection on its surface has also disappeared, making it much easier to read.

A long strand of green grass is tied as a knot through the map, to the south-east of the forest, where the eyes were as the man burst through it. The grass forms a trail along the map, wound and tied around thorns attached to its surface. Their pattern corresponds to the holes in my body, now frigid as ice. A cold wind heightens the sensitivity as it blows, yanking the map from my grip. It flies up and lands in a tree far beyond my reach where it rustles in the branches. The thorns upon it grow enormous and their weight pulls them to the ground. They pierce a plump earthworm who reacts by standing on his tail end with his front high into the air, the thorns pointed straight out from him, threatening all who might approach. The worm's solid form turns into a thick sappy liquid, releasing the thorns which disappear into the soil.

A piece of grass grows tall, stretching as it crawls towards me, and slips a loose knot around my wrist. By the lead of the grass, the wind twirls me around in a speedy spiral motion, and the grass flies far ahead of me and anchors onto something. I follow the grass for many steps and I come to a part wound along a thorny bush. The grass ties a knot around both of my ankles and trips me into it. I receive the bush into the bottom hole of my body I have had since folding into the map. The hole fills and the bush settles into the blood that is dripping from the thorns. It quickly dries, effectively binding the plant to me. I feel alternating hot and cold, the increments constantly diminishing until they share the same moments and fuse into comfort. After this encounter, the grass guides me to additional trees that fill my physical voids and pacify cold with heat and vice versa…reaching the ideal balance every time, until I am solid again with no holes. Releasing the knot from my wrist, the grass snaps up and folds into the sky. I look up and admire the forest around me, not sure of what my quest is now, but it is surely important.

I walk and walk and see a peaceful man eating fruit, throwing a bite here and there to the worms gathered around him. I walk out of the forest to a vast empty sky and into an open field to gaze upon it. The ground is smooth and grass quickly grows up around my feet, continuing high into the air, showing me my own reflection in its dew as it approaches the sky. It ties a knot into the empty sky, positioning into a figure eight. The loops of the horizontal figure eight begin to subtly shake, accelerating to a quick motion. They break apart, forming the moon and the sun. The sun disappears to my left and the moon rises proud in the sky.

The air turns dark except for the bright full moon and a few rays of the sun that I see on faraway ground. I journey to the rays and pick them up, noticing a paper burning inside. I grab the paper and identify it as a map identical to the one before, seeing my face in the broken line at the top of the map. A piece of the sun ray shoots up through this part of the map, catching it on fire. I pick the rays up in my arms, holding them against my chest as I feel them burn me, and I run towards the north of the forest from where I had come, a bit east of here. I drop the rays on what I know now as the territory of the broken line, seeing a row of black dead plants and trees lined with thick tar. The rays bring life to the trees and the tar melts into the ground which rises up into a tall grassy meadow. I step to the grass, exploring the transformation, and find a crumbled map at my feet. It is the same one but now the broken line is filled and my reflection is replaced by the hot sun, its warmth felt directly from the map.

The wind comes and releases the map, pulling the sun into the sky, leaving behind the life newly flourishing from the sun's fallen rays. I enjoy a piece of fruit on the ground behind a tall patch of grass. I watch the sun and moon flip around the sky, enjoying existence for themselves and for all who are gazing upon them…never overlapping except for just a moment, and never in each other's way. Working together as needed day and night, they keep the grass alive…because from that, any necessary assistance shall arise.

28. Soup for the Wounds

My head is tucked forward as I sip delicious broth from a shallow pool cradled into the Earth, protected overhead by trees draped around it. I have the company of three primitive strong caveman-like humans, two men and one other woman, looking directly across to me from the other side. We sip quietly and it is understood that none of us are to eat any of the substance in the soupy mixture…we may only drink its simmering broth. Various herbs, some that I recognize as white sage and large stalks of yerba santa, along with strips of pine and alder tree leaves, float on the surface. Pea pods and full bodied eggplants bounce through the liquid in the current we create with our slurping tongues. A pull from my chest guides me to a standing position as I look upwards to chill the steam on my face with the cool breeze.

I open my refreshed eyes to see the other three standing around the pool, leaning slightly backwards, supported by a harness. I smell an enticing aroma and look down to see I am harnessed as they are, with thin but strong natural hemp that also serves as the rim of the pool. The harness swivels and now my back faces the pool and my outlook of the area has completely shifted. The harness controls my movement as I move forward into a dry desolate landscape with no trace of life. I see the essence of cuts and wounds floating in the air freely with no form to attach to and I see tears that have already been cried, as the sadness lingers. I approach a lengthy wound, a long slash through a piece of skin that looks as if it has been chewed by the brutal teeth of a machine, dampened in warm blood exposing the vulnerable sensitivity of freshly shaved off layers of skin.

The hemp harness chooses my placement, for I have no control, and I collide into the wound in midair. I move through it like it is a cloud, though it looks three dimensional and substantially solid. As I cross through the wound, I feel it jump onto my chest, rattling it for a moment…like a chainsaw or some destructive machine has punctured it, and after the stinging burn of a stab to my chest, I gasp for my breath and fall…overwhelmed by dizziness. The harness catches me, prohibiting any motion during my quick loss of consciousness that has now completely returned.   In fact, I now contrive the will and strength for each additional step forward as the harness begins to support rather than control me. I turn to see the wound from my chest is again in the air, ready to cling to whoever may cross its path.   I grab a large stick and swing it around in attempt to destroy the bodiless wound that sits hungry for a host.   As I do this the lesion increases in severity, now turning bruised and shriveled with more gashes and fresher blood, so I stop immediately.

Other wounds occupy the air but these I am able to avoid since gaining control of my steps. Though I am able to physically stay clear of them, their heavy presence still rules my attention. I see things like an aerial view of a beheaded neck with an Adam's apple that moves silently begging for mercy…and an unidentifiable piece of skin, likely a cheek, which seeps a multicolored infection of pus out of three holes as if a pitchfork had been charged through it. Wounds of this sort clutter the air, inducing a panic in me that I may not resolve them. I hear a woman cry for her lost child and I hear a man echo in an unseen chamber, proclaiming that he had only ever lied. I try to extinguish these disasters but neither by offering my body as a host to the wounds, nor by beating the sorrow with a stick, have I been able to defeat them.

The harness grows heavy as I work harder to pull it along and the clusters of wandering pain slowly diminish. I turn around to grab the other people, wondering if a joint effort would be more effective, but the hemp support flips me back around at once, not allowing my return. I see a dead man robotically swinging a butcher's knife over his head and back down again, thrashing it into the ground. I turn to move around him, but I am again in the control of the hemp harness. I get closer and closer until nearly sliced up by his knife, as I scan my mind and consult with the higher spirits for a last second solution. A tree dwelling ape with arms longer than the length of his body drops his hands down, encloses my palms into his, and pulls me into his tree…sparing me from the blade of the knife. He does not stop to rest or accept my gratitude, but keeps swinging through the tree, alternating with his hands a firm hold of my right wrist, as his other hand drives us through the tree.

We arrive at the far side of the tree and he releases me to the ground where he leans over to watch me. The harness sits folded open, waiting to catch me, but due to the excitement of the ape, I only now realize I was without the harness since joining him. With considerable force, he throws coconuts onto the ground, making it bounce as if I am standing on a thin board. He throws hundreds of them, and finally the ground ahead falls away, leaving me on a thin perch. The ledge quickly becomes weak and the ape throws an open coconut to my face, feeding me with its milk. I am rejuvenated but the perch begins to collapse, ready to fall down a deep hole where the ground has fallen, slowly detaching from the remaining surface. I slide down the perch and hang freely in the air with thousands of feet below me and in every direction around me except directly behind, where along with my harness, I hang by a thread to the remainder of the ground.

The thin strip of ground I am on at last breaks away, and now there is nothing between the top of the long hemp harness and the open ground except for my freely suspended body, dangling in midair. The top of the harness retracts backwards, shaping into an angle from its unknown origin. The hemp tightens and a spillway is formed, opening a path for the wounds and sorrow that begin to tumble down it. The machine bite wound that I wore on my chest, the beheaded neck, the cheek with holes…the traps of the worrisome mother and the exiled liar and the fear of the lost child…all tumble down the hemp corridor, falling deep into the open space of the ground, forever buried away as I witness their demise. The rest of the visible ground crumbles down, covering the pieces of what has fallen.

I now hang with nothing around whatsoever and see the three people I sipped broth with hanging just like me from harnesses…the woman across and the two men on the sides, one of us in each direction. The ground continues to collapse, filling in the gap beneath us…until the new ground rises high enough from miles below to touch the bottom of our feet all at once. The harnesses unravel from our bodies and fall into a circle around us. A few coconuts roll towards us, stopping to root into the ground where a coconut tree grows up. We each sip from a coconut, watching the wind blow the rest into the space within the hemp circle. They break, releasing the milky liquid which begins to simmer until the solid remnants from the coconuts melt away.   The wind intensifies, pushing glorious herbs that I have never seen before into the mix, and eventually eggplants, pea pods, cabbage and long string beans emerge from the mixture. This time we are encouraged to eat every bite, as the wounded ones no longer need it…

29. Deep in by the Stream

I lay down by the stream under the moon in my usual spot of late and drift away peacefully. Just before passing my consciousness fully over to my dream state, I decide to leave my body to sleep and move closer to the stream. At the edge of the stream, I lay with my feet tops snug against the dirt, my chest warming my thighs, and my fingers grasping my head, fingertips meeting along the middle of the very top of my scalp.   Beginning with my two pinkies, pressure increases finger by finger as the backs of my hands twist into each other and I dive into myself. Pointed toes from directly above come in last after bucking my backside quickly up into the air in a pleasant whiplash of ecstasy, with a neck jerk giving me full rotation ability. I look around 360 degrees one way and again the other, completing the same full rotations in different planes, watching myself from every angle pour into my own head, as it floods with a rush of sharp pleasure saturated in heat. The truest sensation of home and natural becoming comes over me like I am being birthed and dying at the same time all while hugging my mother deep as her womb and riding the highest flight of sexual intensity, all melting into the same ultimate pleasure…never wanting to or needing to leave this state. The tightness of my scalp skin and the warm vibrations underneath it nurture my body, nerve by nerve, as I finish tucking myself inside of me.

Lastly, my head caves into itself, and unable to fit inside, my hair is left on top. As my hair leaves me from above, I fall down a large open area, scraping my back along the only wall in sight. I land in an entangled multi-dimensional maze of metal that I march upon as a commander with a whistle in my mouth which I am unable to blow. I scream instead…the recipients of my sounds are my army, anxiously awaiting orders as they dance in unison, occasionally hitting each other with a rifle if left without a task for too long. When one gets hit by another, I get dizzy, so I am sure to keep them busy. Two small groups of tiny men the size of my foot, one to my left the other to the right, roll down steep hills, and I realize I am slowly raising on a platform, separating myself from the ground and my army.   The men land at the bottom of slopes and start digging profusely, making the pit of my stomach, which must be dug deeper for as much of a distance as I am rising.

A few of the tiny hill men are stuck in branches from their roll down. They help each other out of their entanglements and together, they draw enough breath to melt the branches into a stable floor that can be walked upon. To heal the wounds from the branches, they bend over with their legs straight and hands flat on their new floor. They open their disproportionately huge mouths and bite from the floor, leaving holes that somehow turn out small despite their big bites. The men are sloppy, teeth flying everywhere in mad disarray as they smash their jaws together ferociously. In unity, they fall over into a deep sleep. A man dressed in dark clothes, which I remember putting on him, begins to sing an enchanting song. The fallen teeth on the floor move in the song's rhythm as they gather in lines leading to the holes which the men had eaten. One by one, each tooth moves to a hole, dances in a circle in its edge, and slips smoothly into it…respecting the song in their motion.

Meanwhile the other group of little men, still digging the hole in the pit of my stomach, catch the raining teeth with their shovels and chuck the loads behind them, ensuring they do not go into the pit. The downpour stops right after a man drips his first drop of sweat, which I remember telling him to use wisely long ago. Where the sweat falls, a beanstalk quickly grows tall. The scene is filled with loud voices and clanky sounds around the long lengths of twisted metal that I still walk on. The beanstalk, however, is generating absolute silence around its immediate perimeter…I quickly gravitate to this.

I step to the edge in reach of the stalk and not worried about my balance, I fall forward in a bow, my head looking down directly into the never ending space from which the plant is growing. Remaining in my bow, I exercise my retained ability of an infinitely maneuverable neck rotation and look up to a far away ceiling of people with varying numbers of arms and legs…some dangling freely, some spinning the webs that the motionless ones are suspended from. My rotation next pulls my face forward, as I maintain my firm bow and come face to face with the largest leaf on the beanstalk. It divides laterally into two parts, with an opening in the center like lips with the tongue of a red sticky cactus. The tongue pours from the leaf like thick muddy sand and freezes in midair with the tip of the tongue licking upwards, forming a cup a couple feet below my chin. I feel a belt unbuckle right above both of my ears and a heaping fountain of hard black beans falls from them, down the insides of my face, breaking from my neck, leaving holes bordered by hanging pieces of skin. The cactus tongue absorbs the beans and consumes my residual dangling skin. Its sharp face and sticky tongue disappear as the cactus folds back into its leaf and the beanstalk falls, breaking down to a mound of beans.

The beans fill the pit where the digging men dropped their sweat, and the space becomes full again.

I snap out of the trance the beans left me in, standing on one foot with the other leg extended in front of me and my toes spread, letting small sifts of rock and sand trickle through them. Having enough of that, I slap that foot down to the large metal tube I am standing on and I am flung high into the air. A long time ago I asked a man to stand quietly and hold a large stone…he is doing just that as he tosses me a long thick rope, and tells me he has been waiting for me and that the wax is almost ready. I easily climb the rope upside down with my feet leading and stand directly across from the man, also holding a large stone of my own. Each of us throws our stone directly up, catching it again after it hits the bottom of a cauldron that is hanging from the highest of the metal I can see. Beyond the cauldron there is finer lining, unable to support any weight, with webbing behind that, lining the dome ceiling that bears unnatural corners, confusing the perception of space…it appears to contract and expand in size between the times I can see it.

The cauldron leaks thick wax through the bottom at the sites of our stone collisions. Holding our stones, we join them closely together, allowing the wax to sift through the tight opening between them. It falls down as water, with many men below us catching it in small buckets. Each filled bucket travels with its running man to be dumped onto a long downward tube made of algae, seaweed, and moss, with reeds springing up its middle. The reeds are a landing target for those suspended from the web high above, who are randomly falling. The reeds, well moistened for the creatures to slide down easily, keep naturally wet from the surrounding living plants. However, since many of the men sliding down have multiple hands and feet grasping the surface as they go down, the rings ring out like washcloths and dehydrate.

The bucket men keep running the water from the wax from the stone beneath the cauldron, even after I drop the stone, waking the little men with the snapping jaws who find their way up the reeds, chipping them as they climb, and take our places as stone holders. I reassign the other stone holder to draw back the windows to allow more light in. I command some men who are dancing with their rifles to smooth off the surface of the reeds to prevent them from chipping further.

A large man with an unusual amount of hair gives the dancing men an empty box and fills it with assorted metal from his pockets and utility belt…mostly copper daggers, all blades no handles. The hairy man warns them that what the dagger cuts, must be used again as something of purpose. I yell down to them, repeating the man's words that I know are of extreme value but somehow they hear me first and tell the hairy man that they already know. He leaves with his head down, pulling new daggers from his fingernails, placing them in his new utility belt which is covered in blood.

The men each take a dagger from the box and they are perfectly paired…one man for every blade. They grasp the dagger in the center on the palm of their left hand, with the blade coming out the middle of the four clenched fingers. Gently shaving the outside layer of the reeds, the men turn their daggers clockwise all at once with no discussion. I yell to them to be sure the shavings are disposed of properly, but my voice comes from the one bearing a blood covered belt. The men, understanding, drop the shavings down the holes eaten away by the chomping men. They make sure that none of the reeds stay on that layer, which is now covered with old people unable to move, in a constant embrace with one another. As the reeds pass near their heads, the old bodies rise from the skin on their necks and are carried away by large feline beasts with wings. A beast picks me up with the tip of its wing and I use my strongest grip to stay on. As we get to the window that I commanded open for sunlight, I jump off, seeing that this had not been done. I approach the window to interrogate the man of his non doings and I see him hanging from a string outside the window, laughing uncontrollably…at me it seems. I lean over slightly and notice a long way down the tiny image of a girl, tucked forward hugging her legs, facing a creek. I climb down the string from which my comrade is hanging to get a closer look, and I see the girl is an illusion in a mirror.

From a bulge on the structure I am clinging to, I push into the air and land on the ground in a handstand. In my upside down view of the origin of the mirror's reflection, I see seven of the exact same girl in the exact same position, her heads meeting in the center as if nurturing something, or maybe hiding it. My nose starts to bleed and I wipe it off with my belt, now entirely soaked in blood…and suddenly I am covered in hair and back inside. The skins of the reeds fall on me, landing with heavier force than I expect. I resume my role as commander and give the men positive regards for aiming correctly with acute accuracy on such tiny holes.

The fallen pieces of reed naturally land in a circle, interlocking until they fit together like a puzzle. Once complete in a circle the groups of pieces rotate, some clockwise some counterclockwise, combining together to raise into walls as they turn together like gears. With the turn of each circle I move closer and closer to the walls…until I am entirely closed in by the reeds, building up and becoming more and more complex. The algae and seaweed that covered the reeds falls onto my head and all around me. The same tiny men who have the ever snapping jaws enter the room I am in. There is no room for any of us, so they again bite with deadly jaws and begin to consume me. I leak heaps of blood from the attack, filling the room with it to my knees. All together they fall into it and drown…only their bones remain. I grab the vertebrae of the largest one and brush it past the seaweed mix. To reduce the amount of blood beneath me, I begin mopping with it, painting the sides of the room in my own crimson. I stand on my tiptoes to reach the highest place and the floor falls from under me, releasing me from the claustrophobic encounter. The blood follows me to the bottom, where my blood splashes over the seven girls' bodies, still tucked into themselves. They back away and rise from the red pool at different speeds to different heights, each taking a part of me with them.

Where they were, I see a large snake restrained by many ties of strong rope. Remembering that I am the commander, I feel negligent of my duties and blow my whistle. Back towards the top I find true joy blowing my whistle, and the men building the webs of the ceiling drop down at once, flying down like sparks amidst a large fire they are together creating. Each spark lands equidistant on the rope that confines the snake, aiding him in his release. The snake breaks free and sticks his black tongue out, cupping it around me…he pulls me in and I am again bleeding, this time from the cactus inside of him. Not finding the cactus pleasing, I jump from his mouth and onto his head, bursting with him out of the ceiling. From there, I land in the small opening of a relaxed lower lip. He slithers over the window, down a large face, to the ground…and eggs slide down after him, landing in his coil. The lips of the face come together and blow me…and I identify myself as a flower petal touching the cheek of a girl fast asleep. I climb into her ear, tell her that I've done her days work, and she stays asleep. I roll quickly up a hill and wake under the sun where the moon had just been, my favorite place I've ever slept.